This was never something Paige could have designed. For once, her heart was making the plans.

When the applause in the blues bar hit it took her a moment to realize the song was over. Zach nodded, setting his guitar aside.

Paige realized it was the end of the set as he stepped off the low stage. And an instant later she realized that he was coming to her.

End of the set and he was walking to her in that easy amble.

End of the set and he was intent on finding her.

Adrenaline flooded through her. Her heart hammered in her chest until she swore she could hear the pulse beating in her ears.

Zach came to a stop beside Paige. "Wanna get out of here? I've got something special I'd like to show you...."

Blaze™

Dear Reader,

When I wrote the first three novels of the SEX & THE SUPPER CLUB miniseries in 2004, I never imagined that it would take nearly two years to tell the last stories featuring Paige, Thea and Delaney. I've had a great time hanging out with the club again, and I've had particular fun plotting Paige's story. From the beginning she's intrigued me—such a buttoned-down, controlled woman finally letting a guy show her how to cut loose, and in Zach Reed she's found the perfect man—even if she doesn't realize it right away. It doesn't take long though; something about a man with a guitar in his hands is enough to make any woman weak at the knees.

I hope you'll visit Kristin@kristinhardy.com and tell me what you think. Look for Thea's story in February 2007 and Delaney's in April 2007. To keep track, sign up for my newsletter at www.kristinhardy.com, where you can also find contests, recipes and updates on my recent and upcoming releases.

My very best,

Kristin Hardy

BAD INFLUENCE
Kristin Hardy

HARLEQUIN®

TORONTO • NEW YORK • LONDON
AMSTERDAM • PARIS • SYDNEY • HAMBURG
STOCKHOLM • ATHENS • TOKYO • MILAN • MADRID
PRAGUE • WARSAW • BUDAPEST • AUCKLAND

ISBN-13: 978-0-373-79299-3
ISBN-10:   0-373-79299-9

BAD INFLUENCE

www.eHarlequin.com

Printed in U.S.A.

To Teresa, for the Les Paul
And to Stephen—the fundamental things apply.

Acknowledgments

To Beatriz Ramirez of the Planning Division,
City of Santa Barbara, for answering my bazillion
questions, and to Lieutenant Paul McCaffrey
of the Santa Barbara Police Department
for helping with the details.

CAST OF CHARACTERS FOR
SEX & THE SUPPER CLUB

Book 1—TURN ME ON
Sabrina Pantolini m. Stef Costas

Book 2—CUTTING LOOSE
Trish Dawson and Ty Ramsay

Book 3—NOTHING BUT THE BEST
Cilla Danforth m. Rand Mitchell

Book 4—BAD INFLUENCE
Paige Favreau and Zach Reed

Book 5—HOT MOVES
Thea Masterson and Brady McMillan

Book 6—BAD BEHAVIOR
Delaney Phillips and ?
Coming April 2007

1

"WHAT'S SO WRONG WITH missionary?" Paige Favreau looked around the restaurant table and shook her head, the smooth strands of her blond bob settling perfectly. "If you've got to spend ten minutes staring at a book and half an hour getting into position, it's too complicated. The *Kama Sutra*'s for people who like gimmicks."

Sabrina Costas's dark eyes glimmered with fun. "Yeah, but there's something to be said for variety with the simple stuff. Like doggy-style, say."

"Arf," put in Delaney Phillips, putting up her hands like paws and panting happily.

"No way." Trish Dawson tucked a strand of red-brown hair behind her ear. "You do it doggy-style and you've got your butt sticking up in the air right in front of the guy. Not flattering."

"Are you kidding? It's all just cushion for pushin'," disagreed Cilla Danforth, resplendent in the latest Prada. "Besides, Ty worships your butt every bit as much as the rest of you, at least judging by the way he was staring at it at Sabrina's party last week."

Thea Masterson glanced at her watch and grinned. "All right, I proclaim this meeting of Sex & the Supper Club officially in session."

"How long'd we take?" asked Trish.

"Five minutes. Slow for us, don't you think?"

"That's only because we spent the first four minutes ordering drinks," Trish said.

There were some conversations, Paige thought, that you could only have with girlfriends you'd known forever. The group of them had met in college while working behind the scenes on a play. Days spent slaving over sets and costumes and scripts turned into late-night pizza sessions and bonds that had survived the years.

Paige laughed. "You know, it's been—what?—eight years since we graduated? One of these days we could start talking about other things besides sex."

"Name one that's even remotely as interesting." Delaney looked up as the waiter appeared with a tray of drinks.

"Oh, the state of the world? Religion? The economy? The environment?" Paige picked up her pinot grigio. "Some people would say sex should take a back seat to them, at least occasionally."

"Sounds like you've been talking with Jim the Diplomat again," Delaney said.

Paige looked at her as if she had a screw loose. "Trust me, I don't chitchat about sex with my father."

"He probably disapproves of all of us anyway," Sabrina said.

"Pretty much since the sophomore-year play that had the lead actor standing buck naked in front of God and everyone, yeah," Paige agreed cheerfully. "He wasn't hot on the full-frontal-nudity thing."

"It wasn't full-frontal nudity," Cilla protested. "I designed those costumes out of flesh-colored mesh."

"I'm not sure a flesh-colored athletic sock counts as a costume," Paige said. "Especially when it slips off during the first act."

"That part specifically was not in the script, I'll just point out." Trish took a drink of her Cosmopolitan. "I had no part in that."

"Was it my fault that Perry refused to even consider using double-sided sticky tape?" Cilla's voice was aggrieved.

Sabrina hooted. "You're surprised about that? You know how guys are. Anyway, aren't you supposed to have a special costume for the understudy if you find out he's a different size than the lead?"

Cilla glowered at her. "That was a conversation I had no interest in having, thank you very much. Perry should have warned me that we might have a problem."

"When you're an understudy trying to, er, measure up to the leading man, it's sometimes hard to admit." Paige stuck her tongue in her cheek.

"So it caused a little bit of a stir," Delaney said. "The first rule of marketing—there's no such thing as bad publicity."

"There is when your father's the United States Ambassador to Romania," Paige reminded her. "Of course, I told him that you guys were the perverts. All I did was dress the set."

"You still almost had to quit the play over it," Thea said.

"Things were sensitive then," Paige defended. "The Iron Curtain was coming down, I was his kid. It could have reflected badly on everyone."

Delaney tipped her head consideringly. "What about now?"

"What do you mean?"

"When do you get to stop living to ensure Jim the Diplomat's job security and start enjoying life?"

Paige frowned. "I enjoy life."

Delaney snorted. "You just told us you preferred missionary. Look at all of the two-month wonders you date. What about the Ken doll you brought to Cilla's wedding?"

"His name is Ross and he's a very bright man."

"He's a wonk," Delaney snorted. "Talking with him was as exciting as watching paint dry.

"Maybe he's got other qualities," Trish offered.

"You're exactly right, Trish." Paige raised her chin. "Ross is doing some pretty important work in the mayor's office, even if he is kind of a dud as a date. Was," she corrected herself.

"Was?"

"I'm not seeing him anymore."

"And he was a carbon copy of—who's it?—Marty?"

"Mitch," Thea contributed.

"Mark," Paige corrected drily. "No, Marcus," she amended.

"See, you can't even remember their names," Delaney said.

"So what if I can't? Mark—"

"Marcus—"

"Marcus was six months ago."

"And let me guess—he was the U.S. delegate to Freedonia."

"I don't think dating intelligent men is a crime," Paige defended. "You have to sleep with the guy's head as well as his body."

"And you have to sleep with the guy's personality and body as well as his brains," Delaney countered. "Come on, Paige. You deserve to get out and have some fun. Your guys may be bright boys in training, but they usually have about as much character as tapioca pudding."

"There's nothing wrong with tapioca pudding," Trish objected. "I like tapioca pudding."

Delaney gave her an alarmed look. "Trish, sweetie, don't ever say that at one of those Hollywood power dinners you go to or they'll kick you out of the club."

"Comfort food is all the rage in Hollywood these days, haven't you heard?" observed Sabrina, who had reason to know, as one half of the hottest couples—and teams—in documentary circles. "Meat loaf, tapioca pudding, mac and cheese. Besides, they'd never dream of kicking Trish out of the club, not with the film of her first screenplay hitting the box office top ten."

Paige remembered the premiere and the party afterward. It had started off merely celebratory but rapidly degenerated into raucous singing and dancing. Not that Marty—Marcus, she amended—had wanted to stick around.

Just then Kelly Vandervere, the missing member of their group, showed up bright-eyed and out of breath. "Cranberry juice," she told the waiter as she took off her jacket and sat.

"About time you got here," Sabrina said.

"Sorry I'm late. I was at the allergist and then I had to go home first."

"The allergist?"

"Yeah. Kev and I want to get a dog, but they make me sneeze and puff up, so we wanted to see if we could do anything about it."

"First living together, now a pet? Our little baby's getting so grown-up," Cilla choked, dabbing at her eyes.

"You don't know the half of it," Kelly replied. "So has anyone here ever gotten allergy shots? They do a bunch of tests on you beforehand—pregnancy, infections, everything. Then they draw this grid on you and poke you with little bits of all kinds of stuff to see which square gets red."

"And you found out you're allergic to housecleaning," Sabrina guessed.

"I don't know. We never got that far. I was sitting there in the examining room in my little paper prom dress, waiting for them to do the grid thing, and the doctor comes in and says they can't do it."

The waiter stopped by. "Your cranberry juice."

"Thanks." Kelly picked it up and took a drink. "Says the tests showed up some unexpected results and they're going to have to reschedule on the allergy stuff because I'm—"

"Pregnant!" Delaney squealed.

"You're pregnant?" Paige demanded just as her cell phone shrilled. Impatiently she pulled it out to turn it off. Then she recognized the area code on the display and frowned. "Hello?"

"Paige, honey?" She heard her grandfather's voice. "I need your help."

THE EMERGENCY ROOM smelled like antiseptic and floor polish from the big industrial-size buffer a cleaning staffer was running in the hall. Paige ignored the machine and hurried up to the counter and the admitting clerk. "Hi, I'm Paige Favreau. My grandfather is in here. Lyndon Favreau?" she supplied. "He's been in a car accident."

The clerk nodded and clicked some keys on her computer. "You'll have to wait just a minute."

"Can I just go back? He knows I'm coming," said Paige in a rush. "He called me on his cell phone." He'd said he was fine, but that didn't explain why he'd been taken to the emergency room.

And why he wasn't waiting out front to be driven home, as she'd expected.

At the clerk's glance, Paige smoothed her hair self-consciously. The frantic hour-and-a-half drive from L.A.

had to have taken its toll. The more sober and sedate she looked, the more likely she was to get cooperation.

"You'll have to wait," the clerk repeated. "Please sit down and we'll call you."

It wasn't what she wanted to hear. Granted, her grandfather had sounded in pretty good shape when he'd called her from the scene of the accident, but he was eighty, after all.

"I'm a family member. Can't I just go in to him?"

"Not until we get his approval."

Paige battled frustration and lost. "That's ridiculous. He called me. All I want to do is see him."

The clerk looked at her. "Legally we can't notify anyone of anything without his consent and we've got our hands full with other cases right now. We'll get to you when we can."

Glowering, Paige stalked back into the waiting area. *Ridiculous,* she lectured herself. He was probably fine. To hear him tell it, it had only been a fender bender. Still, until he was completely checked out and had a doctor's release, she wasn't going to be able to completely relax.

It happened that way when your only other living relative was a father who lived permanently overseas.

"Makes you want to strangle someone, doesn't it?" a voice said cheerfully, and Paige turned to see a rough-looking guy sprawled in a chair against the wall, lanky legs stretched out ahead of him on the carpet.

Perfect. Just who she'd expect to run into in an emergency room, she thought, looking at his stubbled jaw. A gleam of white teeth glinted below his black Pancho Villa mustache. It made him look like one of those bandits who'd ridden along the border back in the Wild West days.

Probably waiting for a buddy who'd gotten knifed in a bar fight, before they hopped on their Harleys and headed off to the next biker rally.

"I'm sure they're doing the best they can," she said to herself as much as to him.

He winked. "You could just break the rules and walk in," he suggested sotto voce.

Paige gave him a meaningless smile and chose a chair on the other side of the room. She had more things to worry about than shady-looking men with lawbreaking friends. She picked up a women's magazine from the table next to her and leafed restlessly through Christmas cookie recipes and instructions on making appliquéd throw pillows for every holiday of the year. Even at the best of times it wouldn't have grabbed her attention. Now, concentrating on anything was impossible.

To one side, a group of people who were obviously related sat around a tense couple. She wasn't the only one who was worried about her loved one, Paige realized. From the white knuckles on the woman's hands, there were far worse things going on that night.

"Paige Favreau?" A nurse stood at the door to the E.R. Paige rose.

Behind the door, the emergency room was a scene of controlled confusion. Nurses and orderlies bustled to and fro, carrying basins, pushing gurneys or patients in wheelchairs. Her stomach tightened.

And then she saw her grandfather.

Lyndon Favreau lay in the bed with his eyes closed, looking subdued and uncomfortably frail. His thick, wavy gray hair was disheveled. He'd hate it if anyone saw him looking like that, she knew, and crossed to him to straighten it.

His eyes opened. "What? Oh, Paige. How are you, sweetie?"

"I'm fine. What I want to know is how are you?" No IV,

she saw in relief. No obvious bandages. Only his eyes looked funny, a little glassy and unfocused. "The doctor won't tell me anything until they get the go-ahead from you."

"Tight-lipped bunch here." Lyndon nodded wisely, but his head bobbled a little. "I'm fine. You know me, raring to go."

He giggled and Paige blinked. In the thirty years she'd been alive, she couldn't ever remember hearing her grandfather giggle. Laugh often. Giggle? Never. What the hell was going on?

"Are you the granddaughter?" She turned to see a tall white-coated man with tired eyes and a kind smile. He put out a hand. "I'm Rich Patterson, the staff doctor."

"Paige Favreau," she responded, studying him. He was younger than she'd have expected, though judging by the lines around his eyes, he'd seen plenty.

"Don't mind him," he said with a nod at Lyndon. "He's a little out of it because we gave him some painkillers."

"Painkillers? What's wrong with him?"

"Nothing serious, we don't think." He had a nice voice, soothing. His eyes were hazel, she noticed. "He's a little banged up. He's complaining of chest pain. It's okay," Patterson assured her immediately. "I really don't think it's serious. Probably rib or cartilage damage from the accident, but we have to check it out. We'll keep him overnight for observation."

Head spinning, she listened to the litany. Broken wrist, sprained ankle, CT scan to rule out head injury. "He called me from here over an hour and a half ago and he seemed fine," she protested. And she couldn't understand why so far nothing had been done.

"He is fine, but we just need to be a little bit careful. He's had to wait because we had a car flip on the highway with four kids," he added as though he'd read her thoughts.

The families in the waiting room, she thought immediately.

"We've been busy trying to get them put back together. Now it's Lyndon's turn. This could take a while," Patterson warned. "You might as well go out into the waiting room. It's more comfortable."

"I'll stay here, thanks," Paige said, taking her grandfather's hand. He made a sleepy murmur, but his eyes stayed closed. You did for family, especially when you didn't have much.

Abruptly she missed her mother as deeply as though she'd lost her the previous week instead of twenty-five years before. Pretty and light and full of fun, Caroline Favreau had been a woman who knew how to tease joy and excitement from life despite the constraints of her husband's profession. A walk to the park turned into an adventure; Paige remembered sitting with her shoes off in a fountain while her mother charmed the Prague police officer out of disciplining them. With her natural exuberance, Caroline could always manage to get people to laugh and relax, even James.

Then had come the aneurysm and suddenly she'd been gone. Paige's memories had largely blended into the images she'd seen again and again in photographs. An unexpected whiff of Shalimar, though, could still take her back to walking hand in hand with her mother through the museum in Vienna.

James loved her, Paige knew. And maybe life wasn't as fun and full of the unexpected as when Caroline had been alive, but he'd kept Paige with him throughout the years—she had to give him credit for that. "We're a family, you and me," he always said to her. "We stick together." And maybe that had meant nannies to help shoulder the load, maybe it had meant being lectured to behave, behave, behave during seemingly every minute of every day, but it had still mattered. They had stuck together, except when he'd gone on long trips or been posted to an unstable country. Her haven then had been Santa Barbara and the staunch, equally quiet affection of her grandparents.

It wasn't true what Delaney said about her being afraid to live. She lived. She'd just been raised in a more measured life. The habits of thirty years didn't get thrown off overnight—particularly when there was nothing wrong with them. Perhaps she'd never chased the wild bolt from the blue, but that was because she'd seen firsthand the kind of peace and happiness that came from mutual respect, shared goals, trust. So what if it didn't work for Delaney? It had been something solid and wonderful for Paige's grandparents and even her parents. And Paige believed it was out there for her.

She liked order, predictability. If she preferred guys like Rich Patterson to the Frito Bandito out in the lobby, it was because they were doing something with their lives. They were attempting to make a difference in the world. If she'd yet to find true love among the dry discussions, someone who made her pulse beat faster, that was her business, right?

And if somewhere deep down she wondered if she was going to be sorry at the end of her life that she'd lived so quietly, that was her business, too.

The time dragged by, with the orderlies bustling in to take her grandfather off for tests and then return, and the doctor coming back to put on the cast. When she saw the hot-pink roll of fiberglass in his hand, she stopped him. "Not that. He'd much rather have the clear kind, trust me."

"Sorry. We've kind of had a run on casting material. Central Services hasn't had a chance to restock."

"Not even blue or green?" Though those would scarcely be the choice of her understated grandfather.

"How about pink or pink? I wish we had something else

to offer, but we don't right now. He picked a bad day to break something. He can put a sock over it, though."

"Oh, trust me, he will," she said.

Lyndon's eyes fluttered but didn't open, so Paige gave in. And the doctor left and the waiting went on. Paige looked at her watch and yawned.

A nurse appeared. "We've got the results of the CT scan," she said briskly.

"What are they?" Paige asked.

"Good news, just like we expected. The doc says he's healthy as a horse, outside of being banged up. Everything came out negative."

Relief had her feeling weak. For all that she'd been sure he hadn't been seriously hurt, there had been that tiny bit of doubt nibbling at her. Now finally she could relax. "That's great. So what happens now? Can I get him home?"

"We're going to keep him overnight to monitor the chest pain. You can come get him in the morning."

Lyndon opened his eyes and blinked sleepily at Paige. "I'm sorry about all the trouble," he mumbled.

"Hush, Granddad." She squeezed his hand. "It's no trouble. I'm just sorry you're hurt."

"We'll get him all fixed up," the nurse soothed. "A nice snooze tonight and he'll be raring to go tomorrow." She turned to Paige. "We'll need you to go out in the lobby and do the admitting paperwork. We've got his wallet and clothing set aside. You can come pick him up tomorrow morning about eleven."

Paige leaned over to press a kiss on her grandfather's forehead. "Take care," she said softly. "I'll be back for you tomorrow."

"'Bye, sweetie," he mumbled. "You have the key to the house, right?"

"I'll be fine," she assured him. "Sleep well."

His eyes drifted closed and she walked away.

Pushing open the door to the lobby, she gave a jaw-creaking yawn. Her grandfather wasn't the only one who was nodding off. Maybe it was the worrying or the drive, but despite the fact that it wasn't even ten yet, she was exhausted. All she wanted to do was get to her grandfather's house and tumble into bed.

It wasn't going to happen anytime soon, though, she saw with a sinking heart. There was a line of people waiting for processing. A *long* line. Clearly getting through the emergency room required a Zenlike sense of calm and more endurance than she was entirely sure she possessed. She gave her name and went out to the seating area.

The families of the kids were gone, probably upstairs in the surgery unit, waiting for word. The Frito Bandito was there, though, in practically the same position as when she'd left, an open magazine in his hands. He glanced up, dark-eyed, as Paige walked toward the chairs. One black brow rose. "Still here?"

"Still here." She sat with a sigh, wondering if the chairs were really as uncomfortable as they seemed or whether all chairs just felt that way after so many hours.

"I figure it's medical research," he said. "They're trying to see how long they can keep us waiting around before we go nuts." He grinned and she felt the flip in her stomach. She blinked. Dangerous, this one. When she'd first seen him, he'd merely looked disreputable. Now she saw the hollow cheeks, the dark eyes, the careless confidence that set something in her blood to simmering.

The bandito set his magazine aside with a thump of finality and rose to walk to the rack on the wall. He flipped through the various issues for a while, and she indulged herself by studying him. Just because she didn't want to touch didn't mean she couldn't look. And he was something to look at, in a rough-edged kind of way. Long and lanky, stripped down to nothing but muscle. Lean, not brawny, a man who looked as though he could handle himself in a street fight. Not the kind of guy you'd take home to the parents, maybe, but something about the way he looked standing there was enough to make her consider revising her policies on one-night stands and unstable men.

He turned from the magazine rack before she realized his intent. Caught looking, she realized with a flush. His teeth gleamed and she felt the flutter again in her stomach. Definitely dangerous. No romance, no sweetness, just pure, hot sex. He wasn't a guy who'd bring you flowers or hot soup in bed when you were sick, but he looked like the kind who could make you come so hard you forgot your own name. He was the sort Delaney would go for in a heartbeat.

He wasn't Paige's type at all.

He hadn't grabbed a magazine from the rack—maybe because the content ran more to *Women's Day* than *Chopper Monthly*. That didn't discourage him from checking out the glossies stacked on the tables. He prowled the room like a big cat, restless, powerful and just a bit threatening. Finally he grabbed a magazine and dropped down into a chair.

Two seats away from her.

Paige swallowed and glanced over at the registration desk, but the clerk was still busy. Then she glanced over at what he held. *"Highlights?"* she asked before she could prevent herself.

That killer smile flickered again, easy, assured. "Hey, after four hours, things are getting desperate."

"If you're looking to 'Hidden Pictures' to keep you from going over the edge, you might be expecting a little too much."

"Looks like I need something else, then, doesn't it?"

Unaccountably she found herself sucking in a deep breath as though she'd been suddenly deprived of oxygen. "So what are you doing here?" she asked.

"Waiting, mostly," he said. "How about you?"

"The same. Exit paperwork."

"Trust me, you could grow old and die first. You can read my *Highlights* if you want."

Without thinking, she glanced at the magazine he held and then found herself staring instead at his hands. Like the rest of him, they looked long and strong, as though they knew how to touch a woman.

And she could imagine how they'd feel. Hot and a little rough on her skin. He wouldn't ask, he'd take—and he'd bring a woman to the point she didn't care.

Paige felt an involuntary shiver run through her and glanced up to see him studying her. "Aren't you supposed to be doing the puzzle?" she asked.

"Maybe I already am." Again the smile. "So who are you here for?"

"My grandfather. He got into a car accident."

"No kidding. My grandmother just got knocked around in a fender bender herself."

Another surprise. No biker buddy, no bar fight. "Is she all right?"

"Nothing she won't survive. She's a tough one. How about yours?"

"A little dinged up. They're keeping him overnight for observation."

The clerk called out a name.

"How about that?" The bandito rose. "And just when things were getting interesting."

"That you?"

"Looks like I'm getting out of purgatory."

"I guess I've got a few more sins to work off."

He stopped and looked at her. "Now there's a thought that'll keep me up tonight." He started to walk away and turned back. "Hey, listen, I play Thursday nights at Eddie's on the waterfront. Maybe you could come by."

Paige blinked. Not a biker, not a bandit. A musician. She looked again at those hands and, despite herself, she was intrigued. Too bad it wasn't possible. "I'll try to do that if I'm still in town," she said.

"Here's hoping you wind up with a reason to stick around, then." And he grinned, stuck his hands in his pockets and walked away.

2

MORNING GENERALLY had a way of making things feel better, even if they didn't look it. Paige studied her grandfather from a chair in his room. A purplish-red bruise blossomed on his left temple, but the blurry, unfocused look was gone from his eyes. Under protest, he'd stayed in his hospital gown and in bed, tapping his fingers impatiently as they waited for the doctor, the hot-pink cast gaily incongruous against the white coverlet.

"Your idea?" He nodded at his arm.

Paige's lips twitched. "I thought you could grow to love it."

"I'm never taking pain medication again. God only knows how I'll wake up next time."

"Look at it this way—it could have been argyle." She grinned, relieved to have him back to his old self.

"I spoke with your father this morning," he said.

"I called him last night before I went to bed. I thought he ought to know."

"I suppose you're right," her grandfather said grudgingly. "But it's not like I'm really hurt. Now he's making plans to come over in a month or two."

"Is he?" she asked, pleased. "It'll be good to see him."

"No sense in him leaving his work. I'm fine—or I would be if they'd let me out of here."

Paige grinned. "I don't think U.S.-Czech relations are going to be destroyed if Dad leaves for a week, Granddad. He cares about you. Besides, if the positions were reversed, you'd be the one dragging me to get on a flight to Prague."

"I suppose. We'll have to see if we can all manage to get together while he's here."

"Definitely. I'll give him a call next week to see if he knows anything about when he'll—"

"Good morning." The hazel-eyed doctor walked in, clipboard in hand. "How are you feeling?"

"All right," her grandfather said. "A little sore but ready to leave."

"I'm not surprised," the doctor said and ran Lyndon through a brisk exam, like a mechanic running an engine through its paces. "Sit up a little."

Lyndon winced.

"Chest hurt? That's the torn cartilage. It's going to take time." He handed Lyndon a prescription. "This is for the pain. They should take the edge off for the first couple of weeks. They'll help with the ankle, too. You're going to want to keep off that as much as possible. Rent a wheelchair and use it." He turned to Paige. "Got that?"

"Yes, sir."

His eyes settled again on her grandfather. "Other than that, you're cleared to go. Just be sure to come back here Friday for a follow up. I assume you're going to take care of that?" He looked at Paige inquiringly.

Lyndon cleared his throat. "Paige lives in Los Angeles. I'll get a driver to take me around."

"You're going to need more than a driver," the doctor told them. "For a couple of weeks, you're going to need help with everything—getting in and out of bed, standing up, sitting down, all of it. You need someone full-time."

"He'll have someone," Paige said assuringly and looked at her grandfather. "I'll stay until you're up and around."

"But you have a business to run," Lyndon protested.

She smiled. "I think my boss will understand." Whether her clients would be prepared to brook a month or more delay on their projects was another question, but she didn't consider staying a matter of choice. For her grandfather, she'd do just about anything.

"I've got Maria," Lyndon said.

"Maria's a housekeeper and a cook, not a nurse. And, anyway, you know it would drive you crazy to have her underfoot all the time."

"It'll drive me crazy to have you underfoot," Lyndon grumbled, but beneath the bluster he looked grateful and more than a little relieved.

Paige just laughed and pressed a smacking kiss on him. "You don't have a choice, Grandpappy. You're at my mercy. Come on, let's get you dressed and out of here. It's time to go home."

THE BIG TOWN CAR purred along the curving road that headed up the bluffs toward Lyndon's home. There hadn't been a chance in hell that he would have fit into Paige's sporty little BMW, and his Cadillac was currently the worse for wear. Hiring a car and driver had merely been pragmatic, and if she enjoyed the luxury of being able to admire the city instead of watching where she was going, that didn't make her a bad person, did it?

Santa Barbara perched between the steep backdrop of the Santa Ynez Mountains and the blue of the Pacific. In the sun that burned through the coastal morning overcast, the ubiquitous terra-cotta roofs gleamed.

One of the comforting things about Santa Barbara was

that little changed. Forget about Spanish Revival, the city was original Spanish, right down to the two-hundred-year-old Franciscan mission tucked away in the heart of town. In most places, a major tourist attraction would be surrounded by shops and restaurants. In Santa Barbara, the mission and its accompanying greensward sat in the midst of homes and quiet streets, even as it had been surrounded by adobes in the eighteenth century.

The mission was one of her earliest memories, walking down the stairs from the Favreau estate, holding hands with her father and mother. The original mansion had been built on the bluffs overlooking the mission perhaps a hundred years before by Lyndon's oil-magnate grandfather. Then the stock market crash of '29 and the thirties had hit, decimating the Favreau family fortunes. Lyndon's father had sold off the main house and most of the land, retaining only the mother-in-law's cottage that he'd built in the twenties—if any ten-thousand-square-foot home could properly be called a cottage.

Only one reminder of the long-ago glory days remained—the gate in the wall between the two properties. Once, it had been open so relatives could come and go. Now it was just a locked door between Lyndon's house and his neighbor's.

He stirred as they drove up to his estate. "That's what caused it all."

"What?"

"The sign." He pointed.

"You got into a car accident because of a sign?" Paige stared at her grandfather.

"I was distracted," he muttered, turning to look out the window. "I didn't do it on purpose."

And there it was, a white placard on the verge before

the neighboring estate that said simply: Coming Soon, The Burlesque Museum.

"The next gate," Paige told the driver and stared at the sign as they passed. No date, no specifics, just the words guaranteed to give her conservative grandfather fits.

"Don't worry about it," she said dismissively. "They can't do it around here. It's zoned residential. I mean, there's the mission and the Museum of Natural History, but—"

"But those don't involve strippers," her grandfather ground out. "I grew up in that house. My grandfather is spinning in his grave right now. Traffic, cars parked on the street, hoodlums. I won't stand for it. The neighborhood won't stand for it," he insisted, his mouth firming. "That woman is not going to get away with this."

"What woman?" Paige punched the security code into the keypad and the big gates rolled back.

"Gloria Reed, that's who."

"Gloria Reed?" She frowned. "Your next-door neighbor?"

"Her and her fool museum idea. This accident was all her fault. She pulled out right in front of me."

"Wait a minute—you ran into your *neighbor?*"

"I wouldn't have run into her if I hadn't been surprised by that blasted sign," he defended. "She just put it up without warning. And she always comes out of her gate too fast. That woman is a menace. Shameless," he added as they pulled into his estate and drove up to the house. "Why, here she is in her seventies and she's taken up with some long-haired kid who looks like a criminal."

My grandmother just got knocked around in a fender bender.

Paige closed her eyes. "Long-haired kid?"

"Appalling for a woman her age. He looks young enough to be her son. Her grandson, even."

"I think he is," she said faintly. The car pulled to a stop before the front door.

"How would you know?"

"I think I met him last night in the emergency room."

"She was hurt?" Sunlight slanted across his face to show a flash of mingled surprise and guilt as the driver opened the door.

"They kept her overnight, like you."

Lyndon opened his mouth, then closed it. "Her grandson."

Paige nodded and got out of the car.

"Well," he said as she helped him get into the wheel-chair the driver brought around for him. "Well," he said again, then was silent until they got inside.

"Do you want to lie down?" Paige asked after the driver left.

Lyndon rose from the wheelchair with a wince. "No bed for me yet. I think I'll just sit down in my easy chair for a while."

"Chest hurting?" Paige asked.

His answer was a shrug; she knew he'd rather grin and bear it than complain.

"How about if I go get your medication?"

"I'll be all right. Just get me an aspirin."

"Granddad, I think there was a reason the doctor gave you something stronger. He said you'd be hurting. Don't you think you should at least take the meds today? Your last dose from the hospital must be wearing off by now."

"I'll be fine."

"I think I'll go get the prescription filled anyway," she said, ignoring him. "Let me get you settled and then I'll just nip out for a minute. I need some things for the next couple of days anyway."

"I don't want to be any trouble to you, sweetheart."

"Granddad, you and Nana practically raised me. The least I can do is help out a little when you're down." Paige tucked a pillow behind his head. "I've been meaning to take a break. It'll give us a chance to have a nice, long visit."

He smiled at her. "You're a good girl."

"I had good examples." She patted his cheek. "Do you want me to have Maria make you some lunch?"

"Not just yet. We still need to do something about the muscum, you know," he said as Paige laid a coverlet over him.

"We who?" she asked.

"We the neighborhood. And you, now that you're here. This estate will be yours one day. Do you really want a parade of thrill seekers coming up here, littering and parking on the verges and looking over the wall from the main house? It's barely four feet high. Anyone could jump over."

"Why don't you make it higher?"

"Because it belongs to that woman," he said. "She refuses to raise it because of the bougainvillea."

The bougainvillea. The bane of Lyndon's existence. Some relation or other had planted it decades before on the far side of the wall. It spilled over the white stucco in a tangle of leaves and blossoms, looking perfectly charming from Paige's point of view.

Lyndon swore at the litter of fallen leaves and blossoms and had his gardener kneecap the blooming vine on a regular basis.

"The contractor told her the bougainvillea roots had undermined the foundation and raising the height would mean tearing out the plants and putting in a whole new wall. She refuses. Completely unreasonable. But she won't get her way with the museum," he said with relish. "I'm going to organize a neighborhood meeting to talk about this."

"Right now you need to forget about the museum,"

Paige told him. "The only thing you should be worrying about is healing."

"We've got to stay on top of her. There's no telling what that woman will do."

"Later," she said.

"We don't have time for later."

"I'll take care of it," she soothed.

"Tomorrow, then," he said drowsily.

Paige sighed. "We'll see."

"I'M TELLING YOU, I DON'T need to be in bed. I'm not made of glass, you know."

Zach Reed looked at the flustered woman on the bed in all of her platinum-blond, buxom splendor and resisted the urge to grin. Gloria Reed was no one's idea of how a seventy-eight-year-old grandmother should look and act. Fresh back from the hospital, she had still found time to put on fresh lipstick—fire-engine-red, to match her acrylic nails. Maybe her days as a pinup and burlesque superstar were over, but she still kept up her image. And she might roll on satin sheets, but that didn't mean she took to being coddled.

"The doctor said you had to take it easy."

"Easy means having a houseboy feed me peeled grapes while he fans me, not having my grandson put me to bed. I can still paddle you, you know."

Zach did smile then. "I bet you can, but let's not put it to the test."

"All I did was get shaken up a little bit."

"Is that why you've got your knee wrapped up?"

She scowled at him. "This time tomorrow I'll be fine."

"Then tomorrow you'll be up. But not today. You don't just walk away from a car getting smacked around like yours did."

"My poor Bentley," she mourned. "Was it bad?"

"Not if you look at it from the passenger side."

"Cute."

"So people tell me. Let's see…he basically T-boned you as you pulled out of the gate, so the front driver's-side quarter panel is pretty much toast. You're lucky you weren't really hurt."

"Good engineering. Those air bags do their job."

"The problem is that he went right into the wheel, wrecked the bearings, bent the axle and did a number on your engine."

"Can I get it fixed?"

He shrugged. "You probably could, and for less than the car costs, but it's not ever going to be the same."

"Sounds like it's time to go shopping, then," she said, rallying. "Do we need to get a new van for you while we're at it?"

It was his turn to scowl. "You're not going to buy me a van."

"Yours is falling apart."

"I'll get one when I'm ready."

"You're stubborn, you know that? Right down to your core."

Zach leaned against the doorjamb and folded his arms. "Can't imagine where I got that from."

She looked at him in reproof. "Disrespectful, too."

"Can't imagine where I got that from either."

Gloria threw her head back and laughed. "It's good to have you here, kiddo. And it was worth a few bruises and losing my Bentley to see the expression on the face of that old geezer next door." A smile of satisfaction spread over her face. "You should have seen him, staring at the sign all pop-eyed, even when the paramedics were trying to get him out of his car. He was having fits over the museum, and they thought he was spluttering because he was hurt." She gave a contented giggle.

"You're a bad girl, Gloria Reed."

"Kiddo, that's been the source of my fortune. Now are you going to let me up from here or not?"

Zach considered. "I'll tell you what. I'll let you up if you can get out of bed on your own and walk over here."

"Fine." She flipped back the covers. Underneath, she wore cream silk lounging pajamas, to go with her silvery blond hair. "Okay, up and across the room." She swung her legs around with a grimace to dangle off the edge of the bed. "Okay?"

Zach merely watched her.

She put her feet down, her toenails a vivid red against the white of the carpet. Her mouth tightened, then she pressed her hands on the mattress and made as if to rise.

"Okay. Done." Zach moved forward quickly.

"You didn't even let me try."

"I saw enough. You're hurting."

She glowered. "What of it? It's just bruising. You heard the doctor—it's nothing serious."

"It will be if you don't leave it alone."

"Yes, Mother," she muttered.

"The mind boggles," Zach said.

"Mouthy," she shot back but lay down with a sigh.

Zach flipped the covers over her. "Okay, you've got your Pepsi and your magazines, and the remote's right here. Is there anything else you need?"

She pouted. "A grandson who isn't a tyrant?"

"Out of luck there. I'm going to go get your prescription filled. I don't want you out of this bed, understand? Now are you set?"

She relented and pulled him down so she could kiss his cheek. "Kiddo, I am as set as I can be. Thank you."

She was no one's idea of a grandmother, Zach thought, squeezing her hand—except maybe his.

THE PHARMACY WAS close and amazingly well stocked. Paige had never really thought before about what you could pick up in a drugstore. So it wasn't exactly Estée Lauder, but she had the basics to tide her over, including a Santa Barbara T-shirt to swap for the camisole and silk shirt she'd worn to the restaurant the night before. It seemed aeons ago now, with all that had gone on. The fact that she'd washed her things out the night before and ironed them that morning didn't help. Maybe in the afternoon she'd take a quick run to the mall and get a few things to wear.

In the meantime, she'd deal.

She rounded the corner of the building carrying her bags, heading absently toward her car.

And saw him.

The impression punched into her before she could take a breath—hot, sexy and just a little bit dangerous. Knowing he wasn't an outlaw biker made him no less disconcerting. If anything, it made him more so, because now she couldn't dismiss those careless dark looks. This time he simply wore Levi's and a white T-shirt, looking lean and stripped down and purposeful as he headed across the parking lot. He'd shaved, she saw, and combed his hair back. When their eyes locked, she felt it as an almost physical sensation. Breathe, she reminded herself.

He stopped before her. "Looks like you survived the E.R.," he said.

"Just barely. I think they should give out merit badges for it."

His lips twitched as he looked her up and down. "Yeah, you probably were a Girl Scout. I bet you had a million merit badges. You look like you'd be good at collecting them."

She didn't bother asking him about merit badges. He didn't look like the type who'd ever been a Boy Scout. "So you're Gloria Reed's grandson?" she asked instead.

"And you're Lyndon Favreau's granddaughter."

"Ten points for you," she said.

"Do you have a name or should I just call you the granddaughter?"

"Paige," she said. "Paige Favreau."

"Zach Reed." He offered his hand.

Not taking it would have been silly, so she shifted her bags and reached out.

And heat flushed through her. The contact felt startlingly intimate, the skin of her palm more sensitive than she'd had any idea it was.

She'd been right about the strength, the hardness, the purpose in his hand. His fingers slid against hers, curved around. Somehow, he felt more immediate than just about anyone she could think of. There was a vitality about him, an energy that hummed through him and into her. Something like butterflies skittered through her stomach.

She let go as quickly as possible.

"Nice to meet you, Zach."

"My pleasure entirely," he said. "So I hear the deal is your grandfather ran into my grandmother."

"We keep it all in the neighborhood, apparently." She swallowed, consciously trying to settle her pulse.

"Convenient. I guess that means you're going to be hanging around town after all."

"I guess so. You?" she asked.

"I was already here for a couple days anyway."

She'd never liked men with mustaches. What was it about his that it only made her focus on the mouth it framed? A mouth that looked more tempting than a man's should, ruddy and sardonic and entirely too intriguing. His brows formed dark, straight lines above those black eyes.

When one of those brows rose in question, she brought herself back to the conversation with a jolt. The last thing she needed to be doing was wondering what it would feel like to kiss him.

"So, um, how is your grandmother?" she asked.

"Oh, sore, feisty. I'm having to sit on her to keep her in bed. How's your grandfather?"

"Bouncing back. I hope I do as well at his age."

His gaze rested on her, warm and lazy. "I think you do pretty well already."

Her cheeks heated. "I thought I was a Girl Scout."

"I always did like those cookies. Melt in your mouth."

And if he kept talking to her in that warm, husky voice, she'd be the one melting. She needed to concentrate on the matter at hand. Paige cleared her throat. "I was hoping to talk with your grandmother in a couple of days about the museum thing. My grandfather is in kind of a stir about it."

"Not right now. She needs to focus on getting up and around. Talk to me instead," he suggested.

"Are you a part of it?"

"While I'm here. Try me."

Paige hesitated, eyeing him. "Okay, how set on this museum is she?"

"What does it matter? It's her house, it's her property. What business is it of anyone else's?"

"A lot. It's got the potential to really change the neighborhood. She lives in a community and what she does affects them."

Zach laughed. "With all the walls and gates that they have? I think the neighborhood will survive."

"How do you know? You're not from this area."

"And you are?"

He was baiting her, Paige realized, biting back the little twinge of annoyance. "I grew up here. People like things to stay the same. They don't like change, especially changes like this."

"Changes like what?"

"Changes like your grandmother's museum."

Zach shrugged. "The neighborhood already has a slew of museums. The mission's at our doorstep. You think one more is going to change things?"

"Given the kind of crowd this museum is likely to attract, yes," she retorted.

Amused, he stuck his hands in his back pockets and rocked back on his heels. "The kind of crowd? Just what kind of crowd is that?"

"People looking for something outrageous, something a little scandalous."

"Seems to me like you could do with a little something outrageous yourself," he said.

A car drove by, startling a flock of sparrows, which flew up out of one tree and dived into the branches of another, disappearing instantly from view.

A faint color stained the edges of Paige's cheekbones. "What's that supposed to mean?"

Zach looked her up and down, studying the tidy outfit she wore. It was the same as the night before, but somehow it looked crisp and smooth again, like she was set for lunch at the country club. Classy, subtle, almost certainly expensive. There was sexuality there, but so carefully packaged you'd almost never see it. Paige Favreau, he sensed, kept everything under control.

He smiled. "Loosen the leash. Have a little fun. That's all Gloria's trying to do."

"It's fun at everyone else's expense."

"Doesn't have to be. She's doing it to benefit a charity, but it could be to everybody's benefit. It could just be that y'all will have a good time with it if you just give it a chance. Come on, don't you think it would be fun to shake these people up a little?"

Like it would be fun to shake her up a little.

"One of those people happens to be my grandfather."

"It'd be good for him," Zach said easily. "It'd be good for you. Live life on the edge."

"I don't think I'm ready for your edge, thanks."

Without thinking about it, he moved closer to her, leaned in close enough to smell the light fragrance of her hair. "Oh, yeah? I think you might like my edge," he murmured into her ear.

Her breath caught. He heard it. She didn't move, just stood absolutely still, not making a sound. He heard a thud as her bags hit the ground. Then she began to tremble, so lightly that he'd never have noticed if he hadn't been practically pressed against her.

And that quickly it stopped being a game for him. The silky spill of her hair brushed against his cheek. Her scent wound round his senses. He could take it further, he could feel it. He could taste her, touch her, take her to a place she'd never been before, and plunge them both into heat and need and madness. But not here.

For a suspended second, all Paige could do was stare at him wordlessly, trying to get her brain working again. They were in a parking lot, she reminded herself, broad daylight, traffic twenty feet away. How was it that she felt as if she'd just come back from somewhere dark and shadowed and intimate? And how was it she felt disappointed?

She swallowed and time began moving again. "It's simple enough. My grandfather—and the whole neighborhood, I expect—want the museum somewhere else."

"And my grandmother wants it here." He smiled. "Looks like we're going to be seeing a lot of each other, wild thing."

She jerked away from him. "I doubt it." She picked up her bags and turned to open her car.

Zach just laughed. "See you later," he called.

He planned to make sure of it.

3

THE MAN WAS ABOUT AS irritating as they came, Paige thought as she drove south on Route 101 toward Los Angeles. Zach Reed was cocky, outrageous, egotistical, obstinate and patronizing. *I think you'd like my edge,* her foot. What she'd like would be to have him gone, him and his grandmother with her wacky ideas. She didn't need Zach Reed in her life. That she'd woken up thinking about him didn't put her in any better mood.

Here she was, driving down one of her favorite stretches of highway on a beautiful morning. She ought to be enjoying it, reveling in it. She certainly didn't need to be getting an ulcer over the headache next door.

No matter how sexy he was.

The highway wound along right next to the water, with nothing between it and the waves but a riprap-covered slope. The narrow beach was deserted at this hour. The sun was only just beginning to peek over the inland coastal bluffs. Bereft of buildings, this stretch was the province only of the wet-suited surfers who bobbed out in the waves, their cars parked in a line on the shoulder. Between Santa Barbara and Ventura, Route 101 was as close as you could get to the edge of the continent without falling off.

And the thought had her snorting in irritation. *Live life on the edge,* indeed. Zach Reed was one of those guys who considered himself the answer to every woman's prayer. Well, she didn't have any prayers for him and she didn't need any answers. She was perfectly happy with her life as it was—or would be if she could take care of Lyndon's concerns about the museum.

And that meant dealing with Zach Reed, no matter how little she wanted to do it. She flashed briefly on that moment in the parking lot, that instant he'd been so close she could feel the heat from his body, when she'd seen in his eyes where he could take her.

Paige shivered. She liked nice men. She liked quiet, respectful relationships. Zach Reed wasn't about any of those. An affair with him would be a wild roller coaster, a thrill ride that would take her breath, her will and very possibly her sanity.

Not that she was even remotely considering it. She ran the windows down and let the breeze come in. No more thinking about Zach Reed. He was already miles behind her. Getting out of town for the morning was the perfect antidote. She'd head home, pick up some clothes, her laptop, the files she needed for work.

If she'd timed it right, she'd hit L.A. just after rush hour and get straight through to her Hancock Park condo. Call it an hour and a half, maybe two. She'd be back in Santa Barbara by early afternoon.

Adjusting her sunglasses, she settled in more comfortably and headed down the highway.

ZACH LEANED BACK ON the couch in Gloria's guesthouse, looking up through the skylights to the overcast sky above. By noon, it would burn off to reveal a blue so pure it hurt the eyes. For now, it was gray and inscrutable. Idly he strummed the electric guitar he held and began to play a blues riff. A two-note riff in E, that classic staple of the blues, that low thud that was the rhythm of a heartbeat, the rhythm of footsteps.

The rhythm of sex.

Without conscious thought, he vaulted off into the high, wailing notes of a solo that he played against the basic rhythm in his head. He played on instinct, fingers stroking the fret board, working the strings, pulling out the keening cries of pain and ecstasy. It was what he'd always loved about the blues— being able to go with it and see where it took him. He was never happier than when he was playing lead over the rhythm laid down by his band.

His band.

What did you do when you'd had a job for over twenty years and you got laid off?

On impulse, he picked up his cell phone and dialed a number. "Creative Music Associates," a woman's voice said crisply.

"Is this Bonnie?" Zach asked.

"Yes, it is. Is this Zach?"

"Bingo. Still trying to reach Barry." They'd become good friends over the past three weeks, his manager's secretary and he.

"Just a minute, Zach, I'll see if I can get him."

He went on hold, listening to the latest White Stripes release.

The phone line clicked. "Jimmy, hey, good to hear your voice, man." Barry Seaton, happy and hearty and slick as goose shit.

"It's Zach, Barry, and it's good to hear your voice, too." Zach could take only sour satisfaction in the awkward silence, given the number of times his manager had ducked him of late.

Barry, to his credit, recovered quickly. "Oops, hit the wrong button. Hey, sorry it's taken me so long to get back to you on that Crossroads thing. That sucks that they dropped you, man, seriously."

Crossroads Records, his erstwhile recording company, which after three well-received albums had elected not to renew his contract. "I'm not too worried about it, Barry, because you're going to hook me up with another company, right? I've already got songs for the new album."

"Oh, hey, yeah, I'm working on it. The blues is a harder sell than it was when Stevie Ray was making headlines."

Zach drummed his fingers. "Nine albums over eighteen years, Barry—you ought to be able to do something with that."

"Come on, Zach, you've been in this industry long enough to know how it works. It's the numbers, man, pure and simple. I don't give a damn how good the reviews are, you've got to move units."

And Zach didn't.

"Get your booking agent—Sarah is it?—have her set up some dates, put you on the road. Maybe I can shake something loose."

"She says it's hard to set up dates without the record company backing."

"She might be right."

"Oh, come on, Barry, I've been playing some of those clubs on the circuit for fifteen, eighteen years. And you ought to be able to find someone who'll take me on for a new album. After all, I make money, we make money," he said, playing the one card he knew would get Barry's attention.

"Look, I'll make some calls, get back to you."

Zach almost growled in frustration as he disconnected.

In Barryspeak, that meant never, and meanwhile his bank balance continued to drop.

He'd gotten a guitar for his tenth birthday. By eleven he'd blasted through every songbook he could lay his hands on, learned all that his teachers could pass on to him and found his home in the blues.

By thirteen he'd joined his first band. He still remembered how it had felt walking into the audition held by a group of guys in their twenties. "What the hell is a kid doing here?" one of them had demanded. "Great, a refugee from Musical Youth," another had muttered.

Zach had just ignored them and plugged in his guitar. Let them talk, he'd figured—all he'd wanted to do was play. And when he'd begun to solo to the backing riff in his head, they'd first quieted, then stared, then one by one picked up their instruments and begun to play with him.

Five years later he'd released his first album. It had been put out by a small indie label, one without wide distribution. It hadn't done much to make him money, but with the pittance of an advance, he'd bought his first beat-up van and gone on the road. When that label had gone under, he'd switched to another. By then, he was touring as the Zach Reed Band. By the time he'd switched labels yet again he'd amassed a critical success and a small, rabid fan base.

Unfortunately small, rabid fan bases didn't pay the bills. He didn't care, for years he hadn't cared, content as long as he was playing. So what if he was in a different city every night? So what if he was piling into his van with the guys to go from club to club on the giant Pacific Northwest blues circuit that ran from Chicago to San Francisco to Portland and Seattle? So what if they ate in diners and slept in fleabag hotels or the back room of a club if they were lucky and in the van if they weren't?

He hadn't cared. But this time his label hadn't gone under—it had dumped him. This time Rory, his bass player, and Angel, his guitarist, had begged off for local gigs. Good reviews weren't enough. They wanted—needed—successful albums to keep their heads above water. And it wasn't happening.

Zach was damned if he knew why. He'd always figured that talent would prove out. He'd always assumed all he had to do was play and make the best albums possible and sooner or later it would come together. Only it hadn't. It hadn't at twenty, twenty-five, thirty or thirty-five. He had a treasure trove of amazing memories, but he'd never quite broken through, no matter how well respected he was. He was thirty-six going on thirty-seven and he didn't have a clue what came next.

Sure, some of the legendary bluesmen had stayed on the road until they'd wound up being broken-down old guys with nowhere to go. He'd played more than one fund-raiser for their cause.

He didn't want to become a beneficiary.

Part of him said to keep pushing until he made it, but in some small, disillusioned corner of his brain he was starting to wonder if maybe that would never happen.

So he'd come to visit Gloria. Here, he could suck up a shot of her feisty energy and have a home base for a couple of weeks while he figured out what to do.

But then she'd gotten into the accident with the tight-assed antique next door. The antique with the entirely too tasty morsel of a granddaughter.

Thoughtfully Zach set his guitar aside. Paige Favreau, so neat and proper, so calm and controlled. She might tell him that she didn't want any part of him; he knew better.

He saw it in her eyes.

It was enough to make him think.

He didn't know what to do about his career, but he did know one thing. Gloria wanted the museum, and that was enough for him. On his twelfth birthday she'd given him a vintage Les Paul. His parents had objected on the grounds that no kid needed a guitar worth a few thousand dollars. What was money for, Gloria had countered, if not to enjoy? She'd believed he was going to go somewhere with his music, and with the Les Paul in hand, he had.

So if Gloria wanted a burlesque museum, a burlesque museum she would get, and Paige Favreau could just be the way to make that happen. She had Lyndon's ear and she looked like the type who could change his mind. And if, in the process of getting her to loosen up and get behind the museum, Zach could get her to loosen up and spend some time with him, well, so much the better.

Yeah, he could do worse than stick around to look after things for a few weeks. And he could put off figuring out what the hell he was going to do with his life.

After all, figuring out how to convince Paige Favreau she wanted him in her bed was bound to be a lot more fun.

Shaking his head, he rose to go to the main house to check on Gloria. They'd always been a likely pair, with the same irreverent sense of the world and exasperation with the rules.

He walked in to find her at the kitchen table, drinking coffee and doing the crossword puzzle.

"You're up and around bright and early," he observed.

"I figured I had to make my move while you weren't here giving me the hairy eyeball."

"How are you feeling?"

"Not bad," she allowed. "I think I'll live."

"I'm glad to hear that." He walked past her, squeezing her shoulder before going after coffee.

"Nona can get that for you," Gloria said.

"I can get it myself." Zach got out a mug and filled it.

"How about a little car shopping today?" Gloria suggested. "I feel like doing a few test-drives."

"Don't see why we couldn't. I like the idea of you in one of those Mini Coopers."

She snorted.

"A pink Ferrari?" he suggested.

"Better, but I'm still going to pass."

"Just a Bentley gal at heart, eh?"

"You know me well."

"That I do." He took a drink of coffee and came back over to sit down. "You know, I'm the last person to tell you to blend in, but have you really thought through this museum thing?"

"What do you mean? You know I'm committed to pulling this off. It's not just for jollies. There are people out there from the business, old people who don't have a pot to piss in. This museum can help."

"Not if you keep going out of your way to rile people up. Right now you've got a whole lot of really excited folks on your hands, and I don't mean in a good way. Maybe it's time to rethink things."

She eyed him. "You've been talking to that stiff-necked old coot next door, haven't you."

"His granddaughter, actually, but I was thinking about this anyway. If you want this thing to come off, you'll be better off playing nice. Why set it up in a way that's calculated to piss people off? Do it somewhere else."

"I locate it somewhere else and I have to pay rent, which cuts into profit. I've got so much room here I'd never even notice."

"You're going to have a fight on your hands to get that variance."

"I don't mind a fight."

The corners of his mouth tugged into a grin. "I know you don't."

"And I like twisting their tails."

"I know that about you, too."

She laughed. "You know it because that's how you are."

One thing he'd come to grudgingly accept over the years, though, was that sometimes you had to give a little to get a little. "Come on, you're smart enough to know that you'll probably have an easier time getting it through if you play it soft."

"I know, but I can't stand that superior look Favreau next door gets on his face. He turned me in for not having my trees trimmed to the exact right height under the power lines on the property frontage. The city came in and practically shaved my jacarandas. And his fool gardener is always chopping on my bougainvillea." She glared out the window at the long, low wall between the two properties, covered on her side with a profusion of greenery and blooms that ended abruptly at the top of the fence as though shaved off with a chain saw.

"Maybe he needs a hobby."

"The man's already got one—being a pain in the neck."

"Is that a hobby?"

Gloria snorted. "For him, it's a career."

PAIGE SAT AT HER desk in her home office, talking into her headset while she simultaneously packed files into her laptop case.

"Yes, I know it's going to be a big delay, Alma. I know you were planning to have everything redone by June in time for Peter's graduation. But it's a family emergency and I don't have a choice."

"I hope you realize what an imposition this is to me," a tart voice said into her ear.

Next time I'll have my grandfather plan his accidents better, Alma. "Yes, of course. If you'd prefer to take the project to another designer, I'll understand," Paige said and crossed her fingers. A few seconds ticked by.

"I don't think I'd feel right doing that," Alma said grudgingly, as though granting a favor. "After all, he is your grandfather."

Toothaches were nothing compared to this, Paige thought. "Great. Okay, I'll keep you posted, but we should be able to get rolling again in about six weeks. In the meantime, we can stay in touch by phone and e-mail and I can have some samples sent to your house."

"Don't forget to give me your cell phone number," Alma said.

Not a chance. "Don't worry, Alma. We'll still be working together, it'll just move a little more slowly. Thanks for your understanding." With a few more pleasantries, Paige disconnected.

And cursed like a sailor until the air in the room turned blue.

"Wow, I didn't know you knew how to talk like that."

Paige glanced up to see Delaney in the door, looking at her inquiringly. "Clients," she said dismissively, pulling off her headset. "The ones I wanted to keep asked to change to avoid the delay. The one I really wanted to get rid of has decided she'll do me a favor and wait."

"Dontcha just hate it?" Delaney asked cheerfully, crossing the room to give her a quick hug. "How's your granddad?"

"Better. Still hurting, and he can't do much for himself,

but I think he's past the scary stage. Thanks for asking. And for keeping an eye on my place while I'm gone. You're the best."

Delaney waved a hand at the sleekly opulent room. "It's no hardship to hang out here, trust me. So you didn't hear the rest of Kelly's announcement the other night."

"Oh, God, right, Kelly. So what's the deal?"

"She and Kev talked it over and they've decided to go ahead and have it. They're getting married."

Paige's eyes widened. "Little Miss Footloose and Fancy-Free?"

"They have been living together for a couple of years now. That's kind of serious."

"Yeah, but there's serious and there's *serious*." Paige thought for a moment and a slow smile spread over her face. "Kelly with a baby. That means we get to be aunties." Her eyes widened. "Baby shoes," she shrieked.

"Definitely." Delaney grinned. "The wedding's in two months."

"Kelly and Kev—who would have guessed?"

"Maybe Kev."

"They're going to make great parents," Paige said dreamily.

"You know it. Anyway, we're cooking up a party for them, so I'll let you know. Assuming you'll be here."

"I'll have to play it by ear right now."

"Where's your grandpa today? Did you just leave him on his own with a few crackers and a bottle of Coke within reach?"

"Oh, he's got a housekeeper to keep an eye on him. Anyway, I'm just down here for the morning so I can get some stuff together. After that, I head out." And, galvanized by the thought, she began moving around her office in hyperdrive, gathering things together.

With a sigh of pleasure, Delaney sank down into her favorite seat—a deeply overstuffed chair in a bronze damask. "So what's it like there? Are you going stir-crazy?"

"Not really. It's kind of nice. I'm getting a chance to spend time with my granddad, which I haven't in a while, and it feels good to be helping. It's actually more like being on vacation than anything. Sleeping in, no meetings, just like a little getaway."

"You need that. You've been running like a mad dog since you went out on your own. You need a chance to catch your breath. How long are you going to be gone?"

"Haven't a clue." Paige slid her laptop into its carrier and added the power cord. "A few weeks, anyway. Maybe more. I want to stick around until I'm sure he's all set."

"I thought you said he wasn't hurt bad."

"Nothing lasting, but he's not going to be up and driving anytime soon. I want to stay and finish the job. Besides, there's this whole other thing going on." She set the laptop case next to a tote bag on the floor.

"Define *whole other thing.*"

"A zoning issue. My grandfather's all up in arms about his next-door neighbor wanting to turn her home into a burlesque museum."

Kelly gave a startled laugh. "A burlesque museum? Like strippers?"

"Tamer, I think. More like vaudeville. My granddad's neighbor was a big star back in the day."

"Who?"

"Gloria Reed."

Delaney tapped her feet lightly on the carpet. "The

name's vaguely familiar. I think I might have read an article on her somewhere, maybe."

"Under *whore of Babylon,* if you listen to my grandfather." Paige unplugged her BlackBerry from its wall charger and headed toward her desk. "Anyway, she wants to start this museum to commemorate burlesque."

"Hey, why not? There's a banjo-picking hall of fame."

Paige stopped. "A banjo-picking hall of fame?"

"Yup."

"The world is a stranger place than we know." She tossed the electronics into her purse.

"You said it. A burlesque museum, huh? I'm guessing your grandfather is unthrilled."

"Try ballistic. He's dead set on blocking it. If I'm not around to work on it, he will, and that's the last thing he needs to focus on right now."

"Can't you just go to the city and complain?"

"I guess. They need a zoning variance to do it at her estate. If they don't get it, no museum. I don't know if they've applied or not. The grandson says it's going to happen."

"The whore of Babylon's grandson?" Delaney perked up. "How old?"

"I don't know. Midthirties maybe," Paige guessed.

"Is he cute?"

Cute was the last word Paige would ever apply to Zach Reed. Ballsy, arrogant and, probably to some people, liquid-metal-hot, yes. Cute? "He's annoying."

Delaney studied her. "You know, a bunch of really interesting expressions just went over your face," she observed. "Spill it, Favreau."

"There's nothing to spill." Paige moved to her bookshelf and started culling catalogs for lighting and furnishings.

"I don't buy it. Come on, what's going on?"

"Simple—they want the museum, we don't. But if Zach Reed thinks he can just push it through, he's got another think coming."

"Really?"

"Really." Paige thumped the stack of catalogs on the desk and slapped some files on top. "He thinks he's God's gift to women and I'll just roll over for him. Trust me, I've got better things to do than to stand around in parking lots while he acts as if he can just play me like putty." She shoved the stack into the tote.

"Whoa. Okay, wait a minute. Start the story from the beginning," Delaney ordered. "This I've gotta hear."

Telling the tale made her angry afresh. And it made her remember just how hot it had been. She dug in her desk for her memory stick.

Delaney watched her speculatively. "So when did this happen?"

"Yesterday." Paige slammed the drawer shut.

"Have you kissed him yet?"

"Delaney, please." Exasperation sparked in her voice. "I want nothing to do with the man."

Delaney began to laugh. "I'm not sure that's going to matter, sweet pea."

Paige scowled. "This is me, remember? I don't go looking for bad boys to rock my world."

"Talk to me after you've been sleeping fifty feet away from him for three weeks. Better yet, call me after you've slept two inches away from him."

"Never going to happen," Paige said.

"Twenty bucks says it will. In fact, I'll *pay* you twenty bucks to have sex with him. It's just what you need. He can be your vacation fling."

Paige rose and picked up her laptop and tote bag. "Just

what I don't need. Quite aside from the fact that it
send my grandfather around the bend, I don't have any
desire to sleep with a grown-up juvenile delinquent. I like
men with brains, remember?"

"So date them when you get back home. Come on,"
Delaney begged. "This is perfect."

"I am *so* not listening to you," Paige said, walking to the
door.

"Okay, don't blame me. I tried." Delaney rose and
followed her. "Where's your luggage?"

"Already in the car." Paige handed her a set of keys.
"That's the spare set. I've already cancelled the mail and
newspapers and put timers on the lights. You know which
plants to water when."

"Got it," Delaney said and looked back at the room with
a broad smile. "Okeydoke. Par-tay."

"No red wine on the white sofa," Paige ordered. "And
if I find one potato chip crumb between the cushions,
you're toast."

"Toast?"

"Toast, melba."

IT WAS EARLY AFTERNOON by the time Paige walked through
the door of Lyndon's house. "Granddad? Where are you?"

"In here," he called from the living room.

"The mailman was out front." She handed him the stack
and set down her laptop. "Do you need anything? How
about if I make us some lunch?"

"I won't say no to a little feed, but why don't you sit
down and relax first? I'll keep."

"I might not, though." She put a hand to her stomach.
"I'm fading away even as we speak," she said with a grin
and headed toward the kitchen. As she got out the bread

4

"SHE'S GOT NO RIGHT," her grandfather railed. "My grandfather built that house. I was baptized there." And he'd never gotten over the fact that it had been sold off after the last great crash of the thirties. Maybe if they'd moved somewhere else entirely it would have been easier. Instead, he'd spent nearly seventy years staring across the wall at the mansion he'd once known as home.

"She's turning it into a joke, having any old Tom, Dick and Harry tramping through it staring at strippers." If he'd been healthy, he'd have been up and pacing. Instead he thumped his fist on the arm of his chair.

"It's not going to have strippers, I don't think, Granddad. Just costumes and things," Paige said. And it showed all the signs of really happening.

"Strippers, strippers' clothing—same difference. She won't do it, she just damned well won't do it." He moved to rise, wincing.

"You're not going anywhere," Paige ordered. "Sit back down."

"We've got to do something and do it quick."

"I'll take care of it."

"How?"

She paused. "I don't know. First, we need to find out

from the planning office how all this works. Once we know that, we'll know how to fight it."

"Fine. You do that and I'll make some phone calls."

"You're not going to do anything but relax."

He frowned. "Do you really think I can just sit around and do nothing?"

Unlikely, she acknowledged. As a compromise, she brought him the cordless phone. "Do you have a neighborhood roster?" she asked.

"Just bring me the address book in the drawer of the phone desk. It's all in there."

He was amazing, Paige thought as she retrieved the book. He had everyone listed. In L.A. she used the same elevator as her condo neighbors, walked in and out of the same front door on a daily basis. She couldn't say she knew the numbers or even the names of more than two of them offhand. Her grandfather, living even behind walls, had somehow managed to get a list of everyone on the street. He'd fought in World War II briefly as a scared eighteen-year-old, but when he'd volunteered for a tour in Korea, he'd been an officer. She didn't envy the enemy then and she didn't envy Gloria Reed now. When Lyndon Favreau set his sights on something, it usually got done.

And if she didn't step in, things were going to get ugly.

So it was later that same afternoon when she stood at the gate to Gloria's estate and pressed the call button. The waning afternoon sun made her squint. Between her trip to L.A. and the time she'd spent in the planning office, the day was pretty well shot. But she knew now how it worked: first, the application for a zoning variance, then the notification letter, then a site visit by the planning commission and the neighbors. After, the planning commission would hold a public meeting to discuss the matter and hand down their decision. Less than three weeks for the whole thing, which meant she needed to jump on things pronto.

The pronto part didn't seem to be happening, though. She stood in silence, waiting for a response that didn't come. The seconds ticked by. She peered through the iron bars of the gate, trying to detect signs of life deeper in the estate, but the road curved abruptly away and she couldn't see a thing. Anyway, the cars were probably in a garage, not sitting out on the drive.

Hesitantly Paige rang the bell again.

She didn't really want to disturb Gloria. After all, barely three days had passed since the accident. The woman was probably still sore and fatigued. Better to track down Zach and see if the two of them could somehow talk this through and work out a compromise. The emergency neighborhood meeting her grandfather had called for the weekend only upped the stakes.

Paige pressed the bell one last time before finally turning away. So maybe they'd gone out. Maybe Gloria was napping. Maybe she was meditating and Zach was inventing the cure for the common cold. No matter what the cause, it looked pretty obvious they were not around.

As she turned to go back to Lyndon's, she heard a snatch of rock music drift out of the windows of a passing car. She stopped, considering. Thursday night. Hadn't he said he played Thursday nights somewhere down by the pier? If she couldn't catch Zach at home, maybe she could catch him there. It wouldn't take long. A quick conversation between sets, a plan to meet later and sort things out and they were done. All she had to do was find him.

And if a part of her felt a little tingle at the idea, it certainly had nothing to do with anticipation, right?

SOME IDEAS WERE better in theory than in practice, Paige thought later as she watched the dozenth bartender shake his head at her. The whole thing would have been easier if she'd remembered the name of the bar. Of course, when Zach had thrown out the invitation, she'd never in a million years have thought she'd want to go see him play. Further proof that the world was a surprising place. The downside was that now it left her walking the waterfront, going from place to place.

She'd already made her way down Stearns Wharf. No sign of him there, which wasn't exactly a surprise. He didn't seem the type to play some glossy restaurant or squeaky-clean club. She saw him more at a tavern, the kind with sawdust on the floor and pool tables in the back. Of course, the Santa Barbara waterfront rents didn't lend themselves to those kinds of establishments, which left her scratching her head.

Okay, so maybe it hadn't been such a brilliant idea after all. But after spending days in the comparative isolation of her grandfather's house, the idea of getting out for a few hours had been irresistible. It had been a nice change of pace to throw on a skirt and some heels and lipstick.

And getting a look or two from the guys she passed was nice, too.

The problem was, she was running out of places to try. Paige walked back out into the warm evening and took stock. She was at the end of the waterfront. There was one more place, probably a long shot, but she really ought to check it out.

Maybe she'd even have herself a drink while she was at it.

The closer she got, the less likely the drink part seemed. But she had a sudden feeling she was going to find Zach.

A flickering neon sign read *Eddie's*. The window held

a lighted sign advertising genuine draft beer. She knew it was the place before she ever got near the door, and when she did, she could hear it: the soft, silky blues with its cadence of sex.

The bouncer sported tattoos that looked as if they'd been done in a jailhouse with ballpoint-pen ink. What the X's tattooed on his beefy bicep stood for, she didn't want to know. Instead she shoved her five at him, ignoring his look, and stepped hastily through the door.

Eddie's was no more prepossessing inside than out. It was cramped and dim, hot with the warmth of too many bodies. Smoke drifted near the ceiling in blithe violation of antismoking ordinances. A trio of pool tables lined the side wall. The band stood at the back. A few people danced—mostly women, Paige noticed. She walked forward, glancing at the stage.

And stopped in her tracks.

She'd always been a little amused at her friends who fell head over heels for man after man. Not the ones like Sabrina or Kelly, who'd found relationships that were real and lasting, but the ones who bounced from one infatuation to the next, the ones who got breathless and starry-eyed talking about their latest "pash," at least until the magic wore off.

It had never hit her like that. Mild interest, yes. Attraction, sure. But nothing overwhelming. Nothing that she couldn't manage. In Zach Reed's case, it wasn't even mild interest, just annoyance.

At least not until that moment when she stood in the dark bar staring at him up onstage.

Then it just morphed instantly into pure lust.

He wore his usual T-shirt and jeans, but under the lights, drawing hot and nasty blues from a beat-up electric, he was riveting. He wasn't a showman. He didn't strut or flail or talk to the crowd. He just stood and played as though he were the only one in the room, his eyes half-closed, his hands sliding up and down the fret board with the same absent grace she imagined he might use caressing a woman.

Agile and strong. She couldn't help imagining those fingers against her skin. How would they feel on her body? How would *he* feel on her body? She swallowed and glanced up.

Only to see him staring at her with eyes so hot and dark they seemed to burn right through her, binding them together with an arc of energy. Her knees turned to water as he hit a hard chord once, twice, three times to end the song.

The room erupted in applause and ear-piercing whistles. She glanced around. A chair, a stool…she had to find somewhere to sit and soon. When she saw an open bar stool, she slid onto it thankfully, mostly because her legs wouldn't hold her anymore.

Zach's mouth curved, giving her the uneasy feeling that he knew exactly the effect he had on her. With a nod to the backing band, he launched into a new number, and pulled her under his spell.

She felt it, she knew it as it was happening. It was, purely and simply, the aural equivalent of sex. Before, the beat had been faster, the solos more aggressive. Now, the pace was slower, a rhythmic pulse that thudded into her system and had her moving to it without volition in the same way a woman's hips moved helplessly to the touch of a man.

And this time, he stepped up to the microphone and began to sing.

He didn't have the kind of radio-ready voice that was popularized on the television talent shows. It was low, rough, with no pretense of finesse. Then again, he didn't need finesse; what the music required, what he brought to it was a grit, a realness, a husky murmur that floated over the top of the guitar licks that throbbed beneath. So he played and he sang.

And he watched her the whole time.

For long moments she just stared back at his shadowed eyes, at his hands stroking the guitar, and felt as though they were stroking her arms instead. His mouth widened into a wicked smile.

And suddenly Paige started listening to the lyrics, really listening. He wasn't singing of how he'd lost his job or his money or his dog.

He was talking about a woman.

He sang of promise, of all the ways he'd touch her, long and slow, quick and hard, tempting, teasing, breaking down her protests. He sang of long nights in the dark, the pulse of desire filling the room, of pleasure like a drug running through their veins. The want, the compulsion, throbbed in the music. He sang a song of seduction in his bruised voice, and beneath it all the guitar wailed like a woman crying out her pleasure. It made her warm. It made her wet.

And it made her want. Watching his hands, watching his mouth form the words, all she could think of was what it would be like with him, to feel him on top of her, against her, driving himself into her as the music throbbed. How would he kiss? How would he touch? How would it feel that first time he slid inside her, the first time she really knew him, before he brought them both to orgasm?

When the applause hit, it took her a moment to realize the song was over. Zach nodded, then set his guitar aside.

End of the set, she realized, as he stepped off the low stage. And an instant later she realized that he was coming over.

Adrenaline flooded through her. He walked across to her in that easy amble, body casual, eyes single-mindedly focused. Her heart sped up until she swore she could hear her pulse beat over the Robert Cray song playing on the sound system.

Zach came to a stop beside her. "Look who's here."

"Hello." She couldn't seem to get her breath.

"This is a surprise." He looked her up and down. "A nice one, by the way. You look good."

To her complete annoyance, she blushed. "You sound good."

"Thanks."

There wasn't a stool near her, so he just contented himself with standing next to her. Uncomfortably next to her, she noticed. If he'd been potent across the room, up close the heat, the sexuality, were palpable. She didn't want to want him, but somehow she wanted just the same.

She moistened her lips. "That song was…different."

He gave a low laugh and trailed his fingers up her arm. "You thought so?"

She felt the goosebumps rise. "Aren't the blues supposed to be about being in jail or being down so low or having some other guy digging sweet potatoes in your garden?"

"I don't spend a lot of time digging sweet potatoes. Sometimes I like to be a little more direct."

"You wrote that?"

He rested a hand on the bar. "Sort of. I mean, the basic line is a classic, but the lead's always different and the lyrics are…well, sometimes I improvise."

"Onstage? You mean you just came up with that?"

"Parts. I guess I must have been inspired."

His eyes weren't entirely black, she saw. They had glints of gold around the edges, flickers of heat. There was something mesmerizing about them.

The bartender walked up and tossed down a couple of bar mats, the slap of cardboard on wood startling her. "Get you something, Zach?"

"Beer and whatever she's having," he said, nodding to Paige.

She considered her options. "Wild Turkey, please."

Zach watched her, eyebrows raised. "Bourbon gal?"

She gave a quick smile. "Not really. I usually drink wine, but I figure when in Rome…,"

"Careful. The Turkey can nip at you if you're not used to it. Besides, you don't want some guy trying to get you hammered and taking advantage of you."

"Really? Would that be you?"

"No." He gave a wolfish smile. "I'm going to sleep with you when you're sober. I think it'll make the whole experience a lot more rewarding."

Time seemed to pause for a beat, and for just that time she hadn't a coherent thought in her head. "Yes. Well…" she managed and cleared her throat. "So this is what you do?"

The look he gave her was one of pure amusement. "When I can get paid for it. This is just a pickup gig I worked out while I'm here in town. What did you think?"

What she thought was that the height of the stool put her eyes at the level of his mouth, and she was finding herself increasingly conscious of it.

"Extended silence is never a good sign," he observed.

"I liked it. A lot. I don't know much of anything about the blues, but I think you are seriously good."

"Tell that to my record label."

"What?"

"Nothing. How's your grandfather?"

Her grandfather? She struggled to organize her thoughts. "Um, upset, actually. That's why I'm here."

"I thought maybe you were here for me."

The silence stretched out as she stared up at him helplessly. She'd come here for a purpose, but right now all she could think about, with his thigh pressing against the outside of hers, was of him. When he began to lean his head fractionally toward hers, panic vaulted through her chest, jostling with exhilaration, anticipation, delight.

"Beer and a shot," the bartender said, startling them both.

Paige reached out, grateful for the distraction, feeling like she'd slipped on ice and righted herself before falling. "The variance application," she said, her voice stronger. "My grandfather's organizing a meeting to fight it."

"A lynch mob?"

"I don't know. It just seems like a bit much." The bourbon had a sharper bite than she'd expected; the heat it sent through her, instant. "I don't want things to get ugly. I thought maybe you and I could work it, instead."

"I'd be happy to work—"

"You know what I meant."

That white smile flickered.

"Yeah. So you'll call off the dogs?" He raised his beer and took a swig.

Paige frowned. "No, actually I was hoping you'd talk with Gloria about putting the museum somewhere else."

Zach threw back his head and laughed.

"What?" she asked, taking another drink and sitting a bit taller.

"I like your compromise—Gloria backs down."

"All she has to do is change the location."

"I have a better idea—your grandfather and the rest of

the people in the neighborhood let her do what she wants with her property. The parking will all be on-site. It'll only operate during daylight hours. The signs will be small. How do you like that compromise?"

"I want my grandfather's estate to stay a nice place to live."

"And I want to see Gloria get her museum." His eyes twinkled. "I guess we have to be enemies, Wild Thing."

She flushed. "Don't call me that."

"What do you want me to call you? Princess?"

"Princess," she echoed as though it were an insult.

"Didn't think so. Still, you've said your piece and this hardly looks like your kind of place. Your grandfather should appreciate the fact that you came all the way down here. So I guess that means you're on your way." He eyed her. "Unless you're just looking to see how the other half lives." He raised his glass. "To Paige's first dive bar."

"You don't know that," she countered. "I could go to places like this every night of the week."

He scanned her up and down until her cheeks heated. "Nope, not seeing it."

"Shows what you know."

He rested one hand on the bar and leaned in toward her. "Stick around and I'll show you what I know," he murmured.

There wasn't enough air, Paige thought in a panic. She couldn't breathe, her heart was ready to jump out of her chest and, above all, most of all she wanted to kiss him. No, that wasn't precisely true—she wanted him to kiss her. She wanted someone else to take control of things, because it didn't make sense—he wasn't her type, they were so wrong, wrong, wrong, but God, the thought of it had the breath backing up in her lungs.

Out of the corner of her eye she saw the woman on the next stool leave. Relief made her exhale. If she could just get him to move away and sit, maybe she could think straight again, maybe she could focus on something besides how it would feel to press against that hard, rangy body and have his mouth on hers. "Why don't you sit—"

She turned her head to him—that's all it was, simply turning her head to talk to him—but his mouth was just there, and suddenly it wasn't simple anymore. Suddenly his mouth was hot and hard on hers, the feel of it, the heat of it sucking her down and in until for the first time in her life Paige Favreau couldn't think.

She could only feel.

Heat. It blazed through her, the rush of it like a wildfire. In self-defense, she closed her eyes. And then Zach was all there was, Zach and the wanting, Zach and the promise, Zach and all that good heat. And she gave herself over to it.

He didn't bother with teasing or clever seduction. He just took. Hands hard on her, he kissed her with lips and teeth and tongue the way no man ever had before. He dived fearlessly into it and he dared her to come with him, sliding one arm around her waist, the other up into her hair so that he was all around her, all she could taste, all she could feel.

And all she could do was want more.

Maybe it was the liquor, maybe it was the hour, maybe it was the temptation that he'd presented from the start. She'd always been the good girl, the one who went for the smart, presentable boys. Ambassadors' daughters didn't get caught making out in bars. But, oh, his hands felt so good sliding over her hips, and his mouth was doing mind-bending things to her that made it impossible to really worry about it. She was a grown-up and a woman and for once she just let herself feel and take without a thought for the consequences.

On the sound system, a woman sang about a thing

called love. The seconds dragged by, but neither of them pulled away.

Zach Reed had kissed plenty of women in his time, had had hot, sweaty sex with plenty more. He'd had women whose bodies and mouths sent him into bliss, orgasms that were religious experiences, but always—always—he could walk away. Always he was the master of himself.

Suddenly he was in the middle of something he couldn't even remotely control, something that had exploded with power. It had started when he'd looked up to see her, leggy and lovely and dark-eyed, staring at him with eyes that said yes.

And if he hadn't been onstage, he'd have gotten her somewhere dark and quiet and private so fast it would have made her head spin.

Instead he'd waited, made love to her with the music. Until she'd kissed him. He felt the ruthless punch of desire, tasted the bourbon on her tongue as it slicked against his. That scent of hers wound into his brain until he was dizzy with it, that scent that had him thinking of touching her, warm and naked in the moonlight. And she didn't just take, she demanded, pressing up against him, making that little growling sound in her throat that spoke to every inch of him.

He'd had no idea. He'd speculated that there was something uninhibited, hidden, under that controlled exterior, but now he was sure of it, and the reality had him granite-hard and struggling for control. It was impossible to say what was more arousing—the intensity of her response or the fact that it was so unexpected.

"Uh, dude, you want another?"

It took a moment for Zach to register the words, then he broke the kiss and glanced over to see the bartender looking steadily at him.

"'Bout time for your last set, isn't it?"

Eyes on Paige, Zach let out a long breath. "Yeah, I guess it's that time."

He heard the bartender walk away, but he didn't bother to look. Paige stared at him, her eyes dark, her lips swollen. From his, he realized, and the thought had the want blazing through him again. She sat there so calm and composed, but he knew what was in her, knew what he could do.

Knew where he could take her.

"This set ends in half an hour. You sticking around?"

She rose. "I should go. Definitely."

"So you're just going to walk away? After that?"

"Yeah," she said. "I think it's time."

"Not quite," he said. Not before he had one more taste. It was quick, hard and blindingly memorable, sort of the jolt and heat of a lightning flash maybe. And then he was letting her loose to walk away without even a word.

If they'd been somewhere else, anywhere else, he'd have taken it further. Standing in the middle of a bar where he had a gig probably wasn't the best venue for tearing off her clothes and going at it.

Just as well; a few minutes more and he'd be whimpering for her—and he still had some dignity left.

He hoped.

Before, he'd been entertained, a little challenged. He'd speculated about her, but now he knew.

And knowing that was going to keep him awake for a very long time.

5

THE AUTOMATIC DOORS swept open as Paige wheeled Lyndon into the clinic.

"I don't see why you couldn't just drop me off in front," he groused. "I can still walk, you know. I could make it if I took it slow."

"I'm sure you could, but the doctor wanted you to stay off your feet, and I don't think he'd be thrilled if you hurt yourself walking right before your checkup." She steered him past the waiting-area chairs and stopped at a clear spot.

"They're only doing this to protect themselves."

"Hey, the last thing I want is a smackdown from Dr. Patterson about not watching out for you. It was my assignment, remember?"

"Which is ridiculous. I'm a grown man."

"I'll refrain from stating the obvious," Paige said drily.

He snapped his head around to stare at her. "You watch that, missy."

"Who, me? I didn't say a thing."

"Hmph." He subsided, folding his arms over his chest.

"I'm going to leave you here and go stand in line to check you in," she said, setting the brakes on his chair. "You going to be okay?"

At his nod, she headed over to the counter. She shouldn't have been even remotely surprised at once again finding herself standing in line. At least this time she knew where her grandfather was and how he was and that everything was going to be all right. Waiting was easier when she wasn't worried sick.

Paige turned to glance around the lobby. It was amazing how things could change in a matter of days. Monday, she'd been living in L.A., blithely unaware that life was going to go on a detour. Then she'd driven north in a panicked frenzy to sit in this very room with a man who alarmed her, the same man who would wind up half seducing her with his guitar just two days later.

Because—she had to face it—if they hadn't been interrupted and they hadn't been in public, she had no idea just how far they'd have gone.

And the thought still gave her butterflies in her stomach.

She heard a metallic chunking noise and the door from the examining rooms opened. And out stepped Zach Reed, pushing the person she assumed was Gloria before him.

Paige had expected someone blowsy and hard-edged, bone-deep tacky. Instead Gloria looked bright-eyed and feisty and more than a little fetching. With a glance that looked very close to devilish, Zach pushed her to a stop near Lyndon and turned toward Paige.

Oh, hell, was her first thought. She should have realized that they'd be here on the same day. She should have figured out a way to be sure they wouldn't overlap, because the last, absolutely last person she wanted to see just then was Zach Reed, not when she still hadn't managed to figure out what she thought about the night before. It had been a good kiss—okay, a great kiss—but, really, she'd been out of her mind. With all that lay between them, what the hell had she been thinking of, sticking her tongue down Zach Reed's throat in public?

Then he walked up and looked at her with those hot, dark eyes, and suddenly she knew exactly what she'd been thinking.

"Hey, Wild Thing," he murmured.

She glowered at him. "I told you not to call me that."

"Yeah, but I like the way it makes you grind your teeth."

"You're a sick man," she muttered.

"Good thing I'm in a hospital. I take it you made it home safe last night?"

"Once I got out of the bar, I was fine."

His grin widened. "I thought you were pretty fine inside the bar. I thought we both were."

"Yeah, well, there was that." And the sober, intelligent Paige was ready to leave it alone—appallingly bad judgment, interesting memories. The problem was that there was another part of her that wasn't so ready to let it go. A part of her wondered, oh, pretty well incessantly, what would have happened next. If she were going to live a fantasy, she supposed that now, when she was on a vacation of sorts, was the time to do it.

If she were going to.

Paige cleared her throat. "So are you guys here for the checkup or is there something wrong?"

"Nope, Gloria's okay." He turned back to survey his grandmother where she sat beside Lyndon. "At least I think she is. I don't know about your grandfather, though."

Lyndon, in fact, looked distinctly dyspeptic. The sooner Paige could separate the two of them, the better. "How long until you can get my grandfather in?" she asked the admitting clerk. "I think something is disagreeing with him."

IN ACTUAL FACT, GLORIA Reed was disagreeing with him, but that was no surprise. She couldn't imagine anyone the humorless old geezer did agree with, except maybe the contrarians. "I was trying to accept your apology," she protested. "I don't know what you're all het up about."

"Because it wasn't an apology." Lyndon sat straighter, looking for all the world like an aggrieved rooster.

"Didn't you say that you regretted that I'd been hurt?"

"Yes."

"And I said, 'Thank you, but there's no need to apologize. Things happen,' which I thought was a perfectly pleasant response. I'm sorry you got hurt, too."

"But I wasn't apologizing," he insisted. "An apology implies fault and wrongdoing."

"My poor Bentley's dead," she sniffed, "and if that's not wrong, I don't know what is. Maybe you deserved what you got."

"It was your fault, too, you know. If you hadn't come barreling out of your driveway—"

"How was I supposed to know you were going to come flying along?"

He drew himself up, affronted. "I drive at a very measured pace, I'll have you know."

"Not on Tuesday, bub."

"It was your sign."

She stared at him. "My sign? What, you read horoscopes?"

"Don't be absurd," he snapped impatiently. "Your sign about that ridiculous museum idea of yours, of course. It distracted me."

She folded her arms. "I think you like ranting about things, Lyndon Favreau. I did you a favor with that sign. Otherwise you'd have to go back to my bougainvillea and let's face it, you've already used up your best material on that."

"What's that supposed to mean?"

"I'm always looking out for your welfare," she said sunnily.

He looked at her as though she were part of a zoo exhibit. "You're a loon," he decided. "That bougainvillea of yours makes a god-blessed mess on my side of the wall, which, by the way, is too danged low."

"Make it higher if you want it. Why's it my responsibility?"

"It's your wall."

"And it's also my bougainvillea."

"Not when it encroaches on my property."

She gave a little snort. "Encroaches? Encroaches?" The snicker turned into a giggle, which grew to a throaty chuckle before she gave in to the deep belly laugh.

"You're making a scene."

She tried to stop it, she really did. She almost had it under control and then the laugh broke out again and she was done for. She lay back, chuckling helplessly, letting it come and come. Finally she stopped, gasping and wiping her eyes. "Oh, Lyndon, you do talk. That did more good for me than all the medicine I got here. You and your ten-dollar words."

"I fail to see what you're laughing at."

"I'm sure. I've got news for you, you stiff-necked old fool—if you'd just leave the bougainvillea, it would add a foot to the height."

He bristled. "The bougainvillea makes a mess, and I want my privacy."

She nudged him. "Why, are you afraid I'm going to peek and see you doing something you shouldn't?"

"I wouldn't put anything past you."

"Watch out or I might start encroaching. Nice cast, by the way," she said, nodding at a patch of hot-pink showing where his hand poked out of his sleeve.

He flushed. "I'm told this is all they had. I was indisposed at the time. I intend to get it rectified today."

"Rectified? I think it suits you," she told him, beginning to laugh again as Zach and Paige came up.

"Are you causing trouble again?" Zach demanded as he reached for the brakes on her wheelchair.

Gloria grinned. "I'm always causing trouble. Lyndon Favreau, Zach Reed, my grandson. Who's your friend, kiddo?"

"Paige Favreau. The granddaughter."

Gloria studied her. "Do tell." She put out her hand to Paige. "Gloria Reed, since Lyndon here probably won't introduce us."

"I resent that," Lyndon interjected.

"Why am I not surprised?" Gloria surveyed Paige. "She's a pretty girl, Lyndon. You did good."

"We're very proud of her," he said stiffly.

"Looks like she's got some spine, too."

"You have no idea," Zach said, giving Paige the kind of simmering look it would have taken a blind woman to miss.

And Gloria Reed wasn't blind.

She pursed her lips. "So are you in town long, Paige?"

"Oh, for a few weeks."

"Perhaps we'll see you around."

"Lyndon Favreau?" A nurse came out of the examining area.

"I think that's us, Granddad," Paige said briskly. "It was very nice to meet you, Gloria. I've heard so much about you."

"I can just imagine. We should get going, too, kiddo," she said with a glance at Zach.

They rolled out into the bright April sunshine.

"Nice day," Zach observed as he wheeled her up to the rental car and helped her get inside.

Gloria gave him a speculative look.

"What?"

"I never figured you as going for the girl-next-door type," she said.

His lips twitched as he walked around and opened up the driver's side. "Just what type did you pick me as going for?"

"The ones that dress in something short and tight."

"How do you know that she doesn't?"

Gloria guffawed as he started the engine. "She's related to that fossil."

"You know, I'd be careful calling someone your own age a fossil."

"It's a state of mind, sweetie. And that man's state of mind is ossified."

"Ossified?" he echoed admiringly. "Don't tell me you're encroaching on Lyndon's territory."

"Every chance I get." She grinned. "How else would I find any entertainment in this burg?"

"You're a bad girl, Gloria Reed."

"So you've told me. So what are you doing fooling around with a girl like that? She's not our kind."

Zach considered. "I thought maybe I'd see how the other half lives."

"Different than us, kiddo, that's for sure. But enough of that." Her eyes gleamed in anticipation. "Are we going to go car shopping or what?"

"One Bentley, coming right up."

IT WAS LOW FOR A privacy wall, threading its way along the property line between Gloria's and Lyndon's estates. Paige supposed she could see why it was a bone of contention, although given the two people involved, probably anything could become a bone of contention. The white stucco rose to the middle of her chest, just about the right height for leaning on. The top was curved.

The remains of bougainvillea blossoms still stained the rounded crest. In normal times, the vines tumbling over the top would have added height, but the gardener's pruning job had lopped off the bougainvillea flat at the crest of the wall, leaving the woody branches chopped off like groping fingers. New foliage was only just beginning to poke up here and there.

So maybe she could understand why Gloria hadn't been thrilled.

Neatly clipped and unnaturally straight didn't appear to be Gloria's thing. Unlike Lyndon's carefully tended concrete-and-box-hedge grounds, Gloria Reed's were vivid and exotic and more than a little wild. Dark purple clematis wound up the trunks of palms, hibiscus grew wanton. To one side, a cluster of bird of paradise sent out spiky orange-and-scarlet blooms. It had the look of some exotic tropical forest where almost anything might happen.

Straight ahead of Paige, beyond a stand of lily of the nile, she saw a figure appear. It wasn't Gloria. It wasn't the housekeeper or the gardener.

It was Zach.

And he wasn't wearing anything that she could see.

Bare chest, bare arms, bare…well, everything, at least down to where the glossy green leaves of the plants blocked her view. And what a view it was. His body was as rough as his voice, all muscle and sinew, intriguing grooves and mounds. The light dusting of hair on his chest gathered together in the center to make a narrow line that trailed down his lower belly like a little pathway to debauchery.

He was stronger-looking than she'd expected—solid through the shoulders, full through the chest. She'd have put money on the fact that he didn't lift weights, but then again, maybe in a way he did—given the types of clubs he appeared to play in, roadies were probably in short supply. Hauling amps and soundboards from show to show might make a good substitute for barbells.

She knew she should look away. After all, if the man was walking around buck naked, he obviously assumed he was alone.

Then again, she had a feeling that Zach Reed did what suited him whether there were people watching or not. And so fascination won out and she watched, able to look her fill for once. He was perhaps a crosswalk's length away. Of course, a crosswalk denoted safety, and she couldn't think of any distance to Zach Reed that would be safe enough.

He bent and dived and she heard a splash. A pool, she realized. No wonder he was stripped down—he was doing laps. For a moment she imagined what it would be like, cool and slick, the water rushing over her skin, teasing her naked body.

Absently she raised her fingers to her lips. She'd fallen asleep the night before thinking about how it might be with him and woken up imagining the same. Running into him at the clinic hadn't helped. Seeing him now only made her want. No, doing something about it wouldn't be smart, but she'd be a fool and a liar to say she didn't want to.

And Paige didn't believe in lying—to herself or anyone else.

She had a choice, though. For now, that choice was to stay responsible and keep her distance, at least until the museum matter was worked out. After that she'd play it by ear. As Delaney had said, she was on vacation and the normal rules didn't apply.

Delaney had also offered her twenty bucks if she slept with him. Double bonus, Paige thought.

She smoothed her hand across the rough stucco of the wall and reached over to pull a bougainvillea blossom from Gloria's side of the property. If only she could figure out an answer to the museum question that would make everybody happy, she thought, studying the tiny white flower amid the vivid pink petals. Then she could just wait around for her grandfather to recover. He'd be satisfied, Gloria would be satisfied and, at the end, with luck, Paige would be satisfied, too. Raising the flower to her nose, she breathed in its scent.

And jumped at the sight of Zach Reed walking straight toward her.

The metronomic splashing had ended without her noticing, she realized. And apparently he'd seen her. Fleeing would look ridiculous, and there was no reason she should. After all, she was on her grandfather's property. She had every right to be there. Why shouldn't she be touring the grounds? And if that brought her to the wall when he happened to be swimming, so be it.

"Peeping Paige? When I told you to let your inner wild thing out, I didn't realize it would happen so soon," he said, grinning impudently as he stopped before her.

"Maybe I'm the lifeguard." He wore trunks hanging low on his hips, she now saw, once brown maybe, now faded to a gold that matched his tan. She tried not to stare at the drops of water trickling down his chest.

"Maybe I should go back into the pool so you can come rescue me and give me mouth-to-mouth."

"Keep dreaming."

"Oh, I do," he assured her. "They've been pretty interesting. You're a lot louder than I'd have expected."

She wasn't going to be amused, she told herself. "Yeah, well, when I call for help, I tend to get that way."

"Oh, trust me, you haven't been calling for help. You've been having a good time. A really good time. Why don't you come through this gate here and I'll show you."

"It's locked."

He stepped up to look down on the padlock Lyndon had in place. "What, is your grandfather afraid Gloria's going to invade?"

When Paige had been a child, there had been a gate of curving, sinuous wrought iron, painted white. It had been the kind of gate that evoked images of fairies and magic. Now the gate was a composite plastic made to look like wood, solid and forbidding.

"I think he's just security-conscious."

"Trying to protect his granddaughter's virtue?"

"His granddaughter is perfectly capable of protecting her own virtue, thank you very much."

"You didn't seem so interested in protecting your virtue last night."

She made an impatient noise and he grinned at her. "Oh, come on, you're not going to say it was a mistake or you had too much to drink or whatever, are you? That kiss was truly something."

Cornered, she thought. "You're right, it was. And, no, I'm not chalking it up to the bourbon."

"But you're chalking it up to something."

"Maybe it was curiosity." She raised her chin defiantly.

"Are you feeling curious again?" he asked, his gaze drifting down to her mouth. "I'm happy to help any way I can. Especially if your curiosity extends to how it would feel if we got naked and—"

"My curiosity is satisfied for the time being," she interrupted. Maybe, just maybe she could figure out a way to do this in her own time, in her own way. Granted, most women had their wild flings when they were eighteen or twenty; that didn't mean she couldn't have one late. She wasn't on vacation, but she might as well be. She wasn't focusing on real life, she was focusing on her grandfather.

Her grandfather.

Lyndon would have a stroke, she thought, closing her eyes.

"I need to go," she said briskly, opening them again.

Zach folded his arms and leaned them on top of the gate. "You say that a lot."

"Just trying to keep my mystique for you," she said.

"You're doing a hell of a job."

"Thank you. I'll see you later."

He snaked his hand over the gate and caught her wrist. For a moment his gaze drilled into her. "Count on it, Wild Thing," he said. "I am."

6

ZACH WAS GETTING OUT of the shower when his cell phone rang. He supposed it was the one constant in his life—he might not have a permanent address but he did have a permanent phone number, something that had come in handy over the years. No one could ever accuse him of being settled, but people could at least find him. He didn't disappear off the map.

Although there were times he wouldn't have minded disappearing, necessarily. Sometimes when they got stuck sleeping in the van on the road, isolation seemed like Valhalla.

Towel around his hips, he wandered out into the guesthouse living room and picked up the phone. "Yeah, whaddaya want?"

"Dude. How's it hanging?"

"Hey, Angel." He recognized the voice with a little surge of interest. Angel, his rhythm guitar player. They'd always been a pair, he and Angel, the core of the band's sound.

And Angel's defection, coupled with the record company giving him the boot, had left Zach in his current limbo. But now here Angel was, calling him out of the blue, and suddenly the betrayal he'd felt at the end faded away.

Zach flopped down on the sofa. "What up?"

"Oh, not a whole lot. I just had some time and figured I'd see how you were doing."

"Taking it easy on a Saturday morning. Otherwise, not much. Hanging out, playing a few gigs with a pickup band when I can. Waiting to see what shakes loose."

"Yeah? I heard that Crossroads dropped you."

News traveled fast. "You heard right."

"Sorry, man."

"It happens," he said abruptly, rising to go into the bedroom. "Not the first time I've gone hunting for a label." Though it was the first time he'd essentially been fired from one. He pulled out a pair of jeans.

"You talked to Barry?"

Zach laughed. "I've talked to Barry's secretary." Which reminded him—it was time for Barry's weekly voice mail.

"Hey, I hope it wasn't the band breaking up," Angel said. "We weren't trying to stick a shiv in you, you know? I just had to do something and so did Rory."

"No problem, man. How's that kid of yours, anyway?"

"Miguel? He's good. I got him a little guitar. He's learning bar chords."

"Give it a couple of years and you two can go out on the road yourselves."

"I don't know. I don't think Ophelia will go for that. She says she's tired of the touring. She wants a normal life. She wants me around."

Zach slid on the pants and propped the phone against his shoulder to button them. "What are you supposed to do?"

"Aw, you know, whatever I can. I'm teaching some kids, some lessons Ophelia set up. Working for her dad days."

"What's he do?"

Zach could hear the shrug in Angel's voice. "He's a contractor."

"A contractor? So you're building houses?"

"Office buildings, man. Tall office buildings."

"I thought you didn't like heights."

"I'm trying to get over it."

"Construction…what do you want to do that for, Angel? You're a musician for chrissakes, not a carpenter."

"I'm a dad," Angel said with an edge to his voice, then sighed. "Hell, Zach, it's a paycheck. The music thing wasn't working, no matter how much we wanted it to. Sometimes you gotta wake up and say it ain't gonna happen, you know?"

It was the thought that had been stalking him in the wee hours of the night. "And sometimes you gotta keep the faith."

"I want to wake up with my family more than once every two or three months."

"Yeah, I know," Zach said wearily, rubbing the bridge of his nose.

"Look, you got talent, you got contacts. You don't have anyone to worry about but you. Things'll break your way."

"You just take care of your family."

"I'll do that. Anyway, I should probably get going."

"Okay, man. Stay low."

Angel laughed. "I'll do that."

"Thanks for calling." Zach hung up the phone and stared into space.

You don't have anyone to worry about but you.

Why did that sound like a curse?

ABOUT THIRTY PEOPLE sat in the inner courtyard on the white plastic chairs Lyndon had somehow managed to rent at the last minute. Paige had put out soft drinks and coffee, bagels and cream cheese and fruit, and the neighbors tucked in with enthusiasm. Why just vent their spleens when they could nosh at the same time? she thought, making yet another run through the area to pick up cups and glasses and napkins.

Then again, that was why she'd bought the refreshments. It was probably just her being cranky. Something about neighborhood meetings always made her think of student council and all the petty squabbling it entailed. Tempests in teapots. Maybe it was the hour of the morning, but she had no taste for it. No taste at all.

She'd helped Lyndon print out an agenda. He'd started off the discussion, but somehow things had gone downhill from there. The talk quickly went off the rails to encompass every one of Gloria's transgressions—real or imagined—and everything she might consider doing in future. At first, Paige tried to stay interested, just to support her grandfather. After a while, though, she found herself inching away from the arcs of white chairs and skirting the pool to get to the back of the property.

This far away, the debate was harder to hear, although Paige supposed *debate* wasn't really the right word—every voice in the room was calling for Gloria Reed to be drawn and quartered.

Ahead of her, she saw the wall with its closed gate.

And standing behind it was Zach.

ZACK HAD HEARD THE NOISE earlier as he'd been swimming. When it kept going, he'd figured it was worth checking out. Then he'd begun to listen in increasing anger.

The last thing he'd expected to see was Paige walking up, though. He'd picked her for standing by her grandpa. That she'd walked away said something very interesting about her.

Of course, there were a lot of interesting things about her. For once, he could study her without her being aware of it. She'd had ballet lessons at some point in her life, he figured—she moved with an unconscious poise. She had the face of a ballerina, too, all cheekbones and eyes. Hers were gray and sober, almost too serious for those delicate blond brows. Hair of the same blond curved around her face like parentheses. She didn't go in for any of the jazzy mousse or clips or anything that he saw on other women and she didn't need to. Simple, classic, always falling perfectly.

And he remembered kissing her in the bar, feeling her heated and gasping against him. That was the side of her that wasn't so simple, and he was determined to see more of it.

He could tell the exact minute she saw him. Her footsteps slowed, the chin went up. She wasn't going to stop or turn away, though. He was betting that she'd keep on coming, even if she wasn't exactly thrilled about talking to him. Maybe it meant that she had the guts to do what was necessary or maybe it meant that talking with him was higher up on her list of priorities than he'd guessed.

Either way was good in his book. He rested his elbows on the top of the gate. She wore a pale yellow sleeveless shirt along with a pair of short pants that showed off most of her calves. And a fine pair of calves they were, not to mention the truly excellent ankles that went with them.

Then a delighted grin spread over his face. For she wore a pair of open-toed sandals, and in the sunlight he saw…neat, tidy and ever so slightly conservative Paige Favreau sported herself some fire-engine-red toenails that put Gloria's to shame. He eyed her as she came to a stop before him. "Nice to see that you've got a little something going on underneath that quiet exterior," he said, nodding at her feet. "You should wear sandals more often."

"Thanks for the fashion advice."

"I'm always here to help if you want me to come over in the mornings to watch you dress."

"I'll pass," she said, but he saw the ghost of a smile.

"So are you here to see me or are you the advance scout for the lynch mob?" In the distance, the sound of the meeting rose until some people were nearly shouting. "You'd think she had blood dripping from her fangs."

"She may also have sold a baby or two into the white slave trade, from the sound of things. God. They're just…" She spread her hands helplessly. "Some of what they're concerned about is valid—traffic, noise, litter. But mostly it's that they don't want to change anything. They want it all quiet and controlled."

"Sounds like some people I know."

She flushed. "We're not talking about me."

"But we could be. So are you making a break for it? Come on over. We could go skinny-dipping, work on your wild side."

She didn't answer. Instead she began to wander along the fence.

Zach watched her. "Where are you going?"

"A walk."

It couldn't be easy for her, he realized. She was one of those compulsively loyal sorts. She'd see walking away from the meeting as a betrayal of her grandfather. And she'd brood on it.

So he drifted after her, following along the wall. Back this far, the bougainvillea gave way to a mini citrus orchard. Zach brushed the leaves of trees as they passed. "You've got your choice of sweet, sour or tangy," he said, pointing to the orange, lemon and tangerine trees. "I'm going to go with tangy," he decided and picked a couple. "I figure wherever you're going, we'll need provisions. Where are you going, anyway?"

"Down to the park." In the corner, where the privacy wall intersected the back fence of the two properties, sat a pair of gates that led out onto the bluffs.

"You got a death wish?" Zach asked, watching her dial the combination that released the lock. "Those bluffs are pretty steep."

"Not if you know where to go." She opened the gate and stepped through.

He didn't even bother messing with the padlock on his side, a mass of rust. Instead he vaulted over the wall and followed Paige. He didn't mind following her, he thought, eyes on those neat hips in her narrow white pants.

The stairway that zigzagged its way down the bluff wasn't obvious. He didn't see it, in fact, until they were almost on top of it. "How did you know this was here?"

"My parents used to take me down this way to the mission when I was a kid. Granddad's pretty compulsive about keeping it up, just in case."

"Just in case of what, nuclear war?"

"Just in case of anything. That's Granddad, he likes to be prepared."

"And what about you? Are you a planner, too?"

"I like having things in order," she answered.

"But sometimes you've got to be off-the-cuff, though, too, right? Spontaneous?"

"Sometimes," she acknowledged.

The stairway dropped them at the edge of the broad green park that sat across from the Santa Barbara Mission. Paige headed toward an empty patch of grass and sat down with a sigh.

"We stopping?"

"I'm being spontaneous."

Beyond them, a teenager played Frisbee with his dog, a bandanna-wearing build-a-breed that looked like a blend of Lab, spaniel and plain old garden-variety hound. Under some trees, a collection of girls, maybe five or so, played tag. A banner read Happy Birthday, Dana. Or maybe Lana, It was hard to tell with the wind flapping the fabric.

The scene seemed miles removed from the fierce in-fighting over the museum and even further removed from his life. Saturday mornings weren't about sitting in parks for him. They were usually spent sleeping in to recover from a late set and then driving like hell to the next show.

This neat, cozy suburban scene wasn't what he knew. He wasn't sure what he thought of it now.

He watched Paige take off her shoes and stretch her toes out in the cool green grass. He glanced over. "First colored toenails, now bare feet in public. This part of your wild-thing program?"

"I don't have a wild-thing program."

He dropped down beside her. "Too bad. You could broaden your horizons."

"My horizons are as broad as they need to be." She leaned back on her hands, shaking a sheaf of her blond hair back out of her eyes.

"I'd debate that if I weren't so lazy." Zach said idly, picking a blade of grass. "So you grew up here?"

"Some of the time," she said. "When my dad couldn't keep me."

"Divorced?"

"Widowed. We lost my mom when I was five."

"I'm sorry," he said.

She gave him a long, searching look. "Thank you," she said, sounding almost surprised. "I stayed with him most of the time, but he had a job that moved him around."

"What did he do?"

"He was a diplomat. Is," she corrected herself. "Ambassador to the Czech Republic right now."

Zach raised his brows. "Hang out with kings and princesses a lot, did you?"

"Sometimes." She flashed a smile that about stopped his heart. "I got in big trouble once because I wouldn't kiss the cheek of the Queen of Moldavia. I was five," she elaborated.

"Look at you go," he said admiringly.

"She was old and she smelled sweaty and there was this cakey powder on her cheek. I didn't want to get close to her."

"Don't blame you. So did you start an international incident?"

"No. I got sent to bed without dinner, though," she remembered. "And I couldn't go play for a week."

"I'd say you got the better end of the deal."

The smile flashed again. "Anyway, a few times Dad got assigned to an area that I couldn't go, East Berlin, Romania. That was when I had to come back here and stay with my grandparents. I shouldn't say 'had to'—I liked it. It was like an adventure, with the mission and the beach and everything. Anyway, how about you? Where did you grow up?"

Zach rolled onto his back, studying the leaves overhead. "Everywhere, pretty much. My parents were hippies. Still are, I suppose. You know, living outside of society's expectations, not getting married, all that. My mom makes stuff to sell on the Renaissance Fair circuit. We'd start traveling in April, go through until October. All over the country."

"It must have been like being on permanent vacation."

"We had to work, too. And my sister and I were homeschooled, so we didn't get off completely. But, yeah, for a kid, you couldn't beat it—camping all the time, always being somewhere new. It was pretty cool."

"What about winter?"

"Winters we stayed at a commune in eastern Oregon."

"That could be interesting," she said cautiously.

He laughed. "It taught me how to live without having a lot of stuff," he said. "Handy for my lifestyle."

"Do your parents still travel?"

He nodded. "Itchy feet, I guess. Family trait."

"You must spend a lot of time on the road."

"Pretty much all of it. It's about the only way to get by unless you're a big national act. Not a lot of blues bands fall into that category."

"Why not move to Austin. Isn't that the hotbed?"

It hadn't been for him. Just one more try that hadn't panned out. "If you want to play every night, there's a better blues circuit up in the Pacific Northwest. It just means traveling a lot."

Paige studied Zach and then lay back with a sigh, hands shading her eyes. "Is it hard having everything be…I don't know…impermanent?" She couldn't imagine it.

"It varies. It's like anything else—some days it's good, some days it sucks. Or I should say some nights—that's what it's really all about. Everything else is just killing time, waiting to get on stage."

She frowned. "But isn't that sort of like wishing your days away?"

He shifted to his side and propped his head on his hand. "Not really that different from most people, is it? They spend their days waiting for their shift to be over before they get to go home and enjoy themselves. I kill time when I'm off and enjoy myself at work. And sometimes I really enjoy myself." He traced her fingers with his. "I liked having you in the audience the other night. I liked looking over to see you there."

"I liked watching you."

"I liked kissing you," he said softly and leaned in across her.

She'd thought once that there was nothing gentle and tender about him. She'd been wrong. It was the sort of quick, easy kiss that couples exchanged, soft, not demanding. He brushed his lips against hers as though savoring their taste. At first, she just lay back and absorbed the sensation, eyes closed to the sunlight. Only a hint of insistence beneath it all reminded her of who he was, what he could do. When he shifted to kiss her throat, though, she moved to sit up.

"Whoa, there, Trigger. We're in broad daylight in a public park. That's probably enough."

"So? You never kissed anyone in public?"

"Not the way you kiss."

He sat up, as well. "Then I suppose you've never had sex outdoors either."

"Of course not."

"You ought to try it." He traced a finger over her instep. "Do something wild every once in a while, Paige. Refuse to kiss a queen. Make love under the sun. You might just find you like it."

7

"WE'RE HERE FOR THE site visit," Paige said to the valet at the gates to Gloria Reed's estate. With a nod, he stepped back and waved them in.

It was the first time she'd ever been inside. She'd heard tales about it off and on her whole life, but always it had been protected behind the high gates of the front or behind a wall of foliage. From the mission area below, she'd occasionally caught a glimpse of the buildings, but a glimpse only—a gleam of white stone, the impression of size and grandeur.

It didn't prepare her for the real thing.

The driveway curved through lush plantings, past a sweep of emerald lawn, up to a long, narrow reflecting pond that ran through the center of the access drive.

Her grandfather stirred. "My mother had that pond built. It used to have big goldfish in it. Koi, I guess they were. We gave them all names."

Paige reached out and squeezed his hand.

The car drove slowly toward the mansion. And it was a mansion, not even remotely to be confused with a mere house. Lyndon Favreau the first had apparently been enamored of the great homes of Europe and he'd built a baroque wonder of carved stone and filigreed bronze. The building's two wings curved around the reflecting pond so that the shallow water revealed a reversed image of the ornate facade. Doric pillars flanking the elaborate grand entrance ran all the way up to the third story.

And her grandfather had grown up here.

"It's lovely," Paige said.

"There's a Japanese pagoda out back...at least there used to be. It's been a long time." Sixty-nine years, give or take.

The car rolled to a stop. Stairs, Paige saw, her heart sinking. Lyndon had the wheelchair for once they got inside—even he had admitted his ankle wouldn't stand up to the entire tour. But five steep stairs with no handrail in sight?

She got out of the car. "I'll go see if we can get some help," she began.

"There's another way in without steps," she heard Zach's voice say.

Amazing how her pulse rate could go from normal to double time in an instant. It had been days since she'd seen him, days of tending to Lyndon, working insofar as she could. And days in which she'd realized that here was a chance to break outside her self-imposed limits for a little while. To sleep with Zach wouldn't mean she was giving up her values. She wouldn't be betraying herself if she indulged in a brief affair with him.

She'd be betraying herself if she didn't.

The night before, she'd fought down the temptation to go see him play at Eddie's, to find him. None of that being swept away stuff. Yes, she wanted to do this, but she had to do it on her own terms.

Her terms had no answer for the fact that just seeing him had her trembling.

He'd dressed up for the occasion in a jacket and white shirt over jeans. Except for his mustache, he was clean-shaven. He looked tame, but any woman who thought that would be a fool.

Her pulse bumped. "Look at you, all cleaned up."

"I'd rather look at you."

She'd chosen yellow for the day, a goldenrod sheath with a matching short-sleeved black jacket and spectator pumps. Simple, classic, professional. She'd never considered the dress as being particularly short or snug—at least not until she stood before Zach Reed. Something in his eyes now made her think of undressing, garment by garment, for his pleasure alone.

"So what's this about a back way?" she asked, ignoring the heat in her cheeks.

A corner of his mouth turned up. "Are you thinking bad-girl thoughts, Wild Thing? Because you're blushing."

"I'd just like to get back in the car," she said. "I'm hot."

"I'll say." He looked her up and down. "Tell you what, let me ride with you and I'll show you the way."

"What's going on?" Lyndon asked when she got back into the car.

"Zach says there's an entrance without any steps. He's going to show us."

"I can climb a few stairs." Lyndon bristled.

"Why bother?" Zach asked, sliding into the front seat. "Anyway, this way you'll get to see more of the house."

"Don't know why your grandmother wants people tramping all over her home," Lyndon said.

Paige thought that two small armies could tramp through the house without ever encountering each other.

As to Zach, she wasn't sure whether she was relieved or disappointed that he'd chosen to sit in front. Certainly the back seat would have been a little cozy for all three of them. But the way he'd looked at her had started that slow simmer in her blood, had her imagining the feel of his thigh pressing against hers, the feel of his hands, the taste of his mouth—

"Turn here," Zach directed the driver. "Head toward that portico at the end. There's parking just beyond. You'll be going in through the wing where Gloria lives," he said, turning back toward them. "The museum will be on the other side, kept separate." His mouth curved. "No tramping in sight."

Inside, the walls rose a dozen feet to egg-and-dart crown moldings. Chandeliers hung down at intervals from plaster ceiling medallions in swirling vine motifs. Underfoot, thick carpet cushioned the softly lustrous marble floor.

Without a word, Zach began pushing the wheelchair. Lyndon made no protest; from the look on his face, he was deep in memory. They passed one door that was ajar. "Wait," Lyndon said. "Roll back. Is that the library?"

"Yep." Zach stopped and reached out to push the door open.

And Lyndon simply stared. Inside, leather books lined floor-to-ceiling shelves. A coffered ceiling hung over a floor scattered with leather club chairs and green-shaded reading lamps. "It hasn't changed," he said under his breath.

"What?" Zach asked.

"Later," Paige murmured.

The wing seemed to go on forever. Finally, though, they passed through an archway to the central entrance hall of the house.

As the first thing guests coming in the main entrance would see, it had been designed to impress. And impress it did. Marble-faced walls of dove-gray soared up some thirty feet to the loggia of the second story. Multiple layers of complicated moldings marched around the ceiling overhead, which bore a trompe l'oeil scene of blue sky edged with clouds, with a Greek god and goddess looking down.

"Apollo and Athena?" Paige guessed.

"Ben and J.Lo." Zach winked at her. "We didn't have the money to get it fixed."

Smothering a laugh, Paige glanced to her right to see the steps that led down to the bronze-and-glass doors of the front entrance. Flanking those steps on either side, broad marble staircases curved up to a central landing and then ran up to the second floor.

To the other side, she saw a reception area. If the entrance hall was meant to impress, the reception room was meant to welcome. Persian rugs covered the marble floor. Damask-covered settees and chairs clustered around tables suggested intimacy, bringing the scale of the room down to simple comfort, no small feat in such imposing surroundings. Gloria Reed, Paige reflected, had exquisite taste, whether in design or in choosing an interior designer.

Or both.

At the top of the entrance steps, a group that she assumed was the planning commission was gathered, talking quietly.

"Lyndon!" A tall, hawk-nosed man with a mane of silver hair strode over to meet them. "What have you done to yourself?" he demanded.

Lyndon looked down ruefully at his cast and wheelchair. "Oh, not watching where I was going, like a damned fool. Nothing serious, though. I'll be back up and running in no time." He glanced at Paige. "Gareth, I'd like you to meet my granddaughter, Paige Favreau. Paige, this is Gareth James, a real up-and-comer in local politics."

The white hair was premature, she saw—Gareth James looked to be no more than his early forties. Paige extended her hand. "It's a pleasure."

"Oh, no. The pleasure's mine." Instead of shaking her hand, Gareth raised it to his lips, his gaze lingering on her. "I had no idea you had such a lovely granddaughter, Lyndon."

Paige coughed and retrieved her hand. Next to her, Zach made a muffled noise. When she glanced over, she saw the ghost of amusement hovering around the corners of his mouth.

Lyndon gave her a satisfied look. "I met Gareth when he was an intern. He's a county supervisor and the head of the planning commission these days, isn't that right, Gareth?"

"Not head of the planning commission anymore. That's Charlie Shepard. Hey, Charlie, come on over here."

And that, of course, started the rounds of introductions in earnest. In a moment, Paige found herself surrounded by the whole group, shaking hands and nodding at names that flew by so quickly she hadn't a prayer of remembering them.

"Why don't you come over here with us, Lyndon?" Charlie suggested, radiating bonhomie. "We were just talking about what the Fed's going to do with interest rates in the next six months. Seems like it's all over the place."

"I'll tell you," her grandfather began, "I've been watching the market for sixty-five years and…" And he was off.

It was good for him, Paige thought, watching him wade into the spirited debate. He worried about her being cooped up but he'd been just as isolated. She needed to get him out, perhaps out to the country club for dinner or an afternoon drink.

"Based on historic numbers, the rates are going to go up," Lyndon insisted. "All you have to do is look—"

"You can't judge by Greenspan's track record. We've got a completely new person at the helm now." The voice was calm, female and certain. And instantly all conversation stopped.

Gloria Reed stood in the archway from the family wing wearing a beautifully cut white silk trouser suit that managed to somehow understate her rather considerable endowments. She didn't quite accomplish chic—it simply wasn't possible with her curves—but with her subtle makeup and discreet French twist, she did achieve stylish, professional and classy.

And a timeless beauty.

She walked over to them with just the faintest hint of swagger. "Thank you for coming, gentlemen." She extended her hand. "I'm Gloria Reed."

There was a beat of silence while the planning commission members simply stared, slack-jawed. And then they hurried to cluster around her.

"That Gloria, she sure do know how to shut down a room, don't she?" Zach observed from where he stood behind Paige. Right behind her. "Look." He pointed. "Even your new boyfriend is flocking over."

She scowled. "He's not my boyfriend."

"Good thing. Way too tame for you, Wild Thing."

"I told you—"

"Not to call you that," he finished for her. "Maybe we'll have to discuss that in private."

Like a ringmaster, Gloria managed to get the planning commission and the surprisingly thin turnout of neighbors seated, drinks in hand courtesy of a waiter. When she had them relaxed, immobile and receptive—with the possible exception of Lyndon, and even he looked a little poleaxed—she launched into a summary of her plans for the museum. "Brian is handing around a packet for all of you that contains a summary of the project, including capacity, traffic, estimated numbers and so on. Now if you'll please turn to page one…"

Even a commodious room like the reception hall could be filled. Zach and Paige chose a padded bench out in the entrance area. Paige crossed her legs with a whisper of hosiery. "So Gloria's the tour master. What's your job?"

"Entertainment."

"You're going to play?"

"Entertaining you, I mean. I think Lyndon's buddies will take care of him. We can't have you bored, though. Nice wheels, by the way." He trailed his fingertips up the inside of the thigh crossed toward him, out of view of the assemblage in the great room.

And nerves all over her body rose to attention. "Stop that."

"I don't think so."

He stroked the tender skin again and she shivered. "Someone's going to see."

"Who? Ben and J.Lo? They won't care. And I guarantee they won't tell." He watched her eyes as he touched her and she felt herself melting. "Come on, let's let Gloria handle the crowd. Your boyfriend can wheel Lyndon around. I'll take you on a behind-the-scenes tour."

"Why do I feel like it's a really bad idea to take you up on that?" she managed.

"Because you're a suspicious person." He gave her a bawdy smile. "Come with me, babe. I'll show you things you've never seen before."

SHE REFUSED TO GO TO the second floor on the grounds that being anywhere within twenty feet of a bed—or even a closed room—could be a hazard. She didn't trust Zach.

And she didn't trust herself. Zach Reed had a way of making all her common sense go straight out the window. Something in his eyes when he looked at her, that invitation to misbehave, made it impossible for her to keep on track. If they stayed on the ground floor in the nice empty rooms that were destined for the museum, she'd be safe,

Paige reasoned. Architecture was her passion. And it was sure as hell safer than thinking about Zach Reed.

Somehow, though, it didn't work. Her gaze was aimed at the gilded moldings, but she focused only on the sound of his voice. She walked into a room to study a carved mahogany mantelpiece, but every sense was preoccupied with the brush of his fingertips in the small of her back. She gazed up at the coffered ceilings and all she could do was think about how he could touch her.

And as the minutes crawled by, her nerves shredded more and more.

"Last one," Zach said as they walked into another room on the museum wing. This time the sound of their footsteps didn't echo, mostly because the room was filled with stacks of boxes, with wooden packing cases. A polished ebony cane dangled raffishly from the edge of a crate; a feather boa peeked out of another. Eight-foot-high scenery backdrops turned one wall into a lady's boudoir, another into a Parisian street. Unwrapped framed art stood in vertical stacks against the wall.

"Good Lord," Paige breathed. "What is all this stuff?"

"This? It's the museum exhibits."

"The costumes?"

"There's a whole lot more than that. She collected her entire career, mostly old vaudeville and burlesque stuff. She's got the ventriloquist's dummy from Tuffy McBarnes and a beer mug that Buster Finley played piano with."

"Beer mug?" Paige raised a brow.

Zach shrugged. "It was his gimmick. Everybody had one back then."

She crossed to the stack of frames leaning against the wall and began flipping through them. Posters, she discovered, advertising various road shows. "Some of these are really wonderful," she said, flipping through them. "They have to be valuable. The Coco Latrec Revue. Hollyfield Girls of 1948. The Paris Lido Show."

He stepped up behind her. "Gloria's had a lot of people after her to sell, but she really wants to do the museum. She figures if she can get people in here, she can raise money to help the retired performers who don't have much."

"The Home for Old Burlesque Dancers?" Paige asked.

"Something like that. She's kind of a soft touch, so she already sends money to a lot of people. The museum and what she licenses from it will let her set up a fund to help more."

Paige flipped through the prints, conscious of Zach looking over her shoulder. He reached out to rest a hand on her hip. Heat burned through the fabric she wore until she swore she could feel each of his fingers individually. She turned to stare at him.

"Keep going," he said. "You're getting into the really great ones now. That's from the first show Gloria was booked with," he said, pointing to a duotone poster in red and white. On it, a chorus line of girls danced.

"And that's from when she headlined the Columbia Wheel."

"The Columbia Wheel?"

"The biggest of the traveling revues." This poster showed Gloria sitting on the edge of a bed looking ready to be tumbled right back in. If Gloria Reed licensed the posters for reprints, she could make a fortune, Paige thought, flipping more frames.

"That's a poster for her first club." Zach pointed to a print of Gloria behind a fan.

"And that's Gloria."

Blue sky, green grass. The sun shone down on heartland America. Gloria Reed stood on the bottom rail of a white clapboard fence, looking back over her shoulder to the camera, one hand shading her eyes. She wore shorts brief enough to show a pair of lovely, coltish legs above high ankle-strap wedges. Her plaid shirt was just a shade too tight; her mouth was a ripe red. Her smile bloomed with joy and promise and innocence.

"She looks about sixteen," Paige said in wonder.

"Fifteen, I think. It became really popular during the war, I guess because it reminded the guys of home. A pretty girl will do that."

"Oh, really," she said flippantly. "You an authority on pretty girls?"

His eyes locked on hers. "I prefer women," he said.

And for a breathless instant everything seemed to stop. There was a humming silence in the air—or maybe it was the rush of blood in her veins. His gaze delved into hers. He stood inches away, but she could feel the heat from his body.

Because her nerves were stretched to the breaking point, she turned to walk over to a door on the back wall, partially hidden behind the boudoir backdrop.

"What's in here?" she asked.

"Take a look for yourself."

And she did. "Aladdin's cave," she murmured, awestruck. It was a small closet filled with marabou and sequins, feathers and all the colors in the rainbow. They were the costumes, swathed in plastic and almost entirely filling the narrow closet, except for a tall wooden packing crate that held heaven only knew what. The plastic wrappings crackled as she flipped through them, stopping to examine an outfit in peacock-blue and rhinestones with long studded gloves. Glamorous but surprisingly modest for all that. Vegas showgirls wore far less. A sheet of notepaper taped to the hanger said *Tessa LaFleur, 1934* in a feminine hand.

She smothered a chuckle.

"It's not nice to laugh at a man in a difficult position," he murmured into her ear. "Especially if you're not prepared to help."

"You've got hands, don't you?" she asked primly.

He laughed softly. "Oh, yeah, I've got hands." And then she stiffened. One of those hands was still around her waist, holding her securely in place.

The other one was migrating south.

Paige's eyes flew open. "What are you doing?" she whispered furiously.

"Shhh," he murmured in her ear. "You don't want to make any noise." And then his lips began moving down the side of her throat, soft and warm, even as his fingers worked their way up under her skirt.

They heard the sound of feet walking into the room. "This would be the main exhibit area," Gloria's voice said. "This and the room next door."

There wasn't any space to move away or even to get her arms down to block him, for that matter. The packing crate was hard against her back and Zach was hard against her front. She could feel the swelling of his erection against her thighs. And she could feel his hands slip between, under her skirt, under her thong.

She jolted against him.

"Quiet," he breathed. "They're right there." With a quick press, his fingers wormed their way between her thighs to find her where she was slick and wet and hard.

And lust flooded through her.

"What about fire code?" someone asked.

"Mmm, you're feeling pretty hot," Zach murmured.

She couldn't speak, she couldn't move, she couldn't see. All she could do in the darkness was feel. All she could do was focus on that spot, that one burning spot and the tightening of tension within her.

And, oh, his hands, his clever, clever hands worked at her, one curving around the fullness of her buttocks, the other sliding steadily back and forth, now teasing her where she was achingly sensitive, now plunging up all the way inside. And with each stroke he drove her closer to release, closer until he had to press his mouth over hers to stifle her moan.

"In answer to your fire-code question, we'd be in full compliance." Gloria's voice drifted through the door. "As the briefing packet shows, the fire marshal has already been out to inspect. I've gotten maximum-occupancy numbers from his office, and of course we'll have fire extinguishers in every room."

As for Paige, there was nothing that could extinguish the need blazing through her but that delicious, exquisitely maddening stroke that was slowly driving her over the edge. Adrenaline swirled with fear, excitement and pure dry-mouthed lust to send her straining against him, struggling to swallow the sounds that threatened to rise up in her throat. She didn't give a damn about the museum, about the tour, about the risk of discovery or anything but the orgasm that loomed tantalizingly close, tantalizingly out of reach.

"What about fire exits?" another voice asked. "Is this a door?" Suddenly all thought of orgasm flew out of her head as brisk footsteps headed toward them. She stiffened in utter, breathless horror.

The doorknob clunked as though someone were touching it and everything stopped: the motion of Zach's hand, her breathing, his lips, her heart, and, very possibly, time itself.

"Not that one, over here," Gloria said.

The seconds stretched out. Paige stared into the blackness in panic, feeling the thud of her own heart trying to hammer its way out of her chest.

And after approximately a hundred billion years, the footsteps receded.

Sudden relief washed through her, leaving her giddy and weak. Zach pressed his mouth to hers hard. They kissed with an exuberant urgency borne of the near miss. His fingers stroked her clit, swirling around it, against it, every slick touch drawing flares of vivid sensation. Paige growled in demand, nibbling and licking her way over his face, twisting against him in fevered demand.

She could feel how wet she was, how swollen, as he touched her. There was no subtlety, no coyness as he brought her back up to a fever pitch. He was hard, relentless. Then he pressed his finger up inside her where she was empty and needy, and it was that that sent her over, twisting against him as he muffled her faint cries with his mouth, even as the group walked out of the room.

It took long moments for the shudders to end. It took more for her pulse to settle as she sagged against him on legs too weak to hold her.

Finally she swallowed. "Wow," she managed.

"You ain't seen nothin' yet," Zach murmured, cracking open the door. "You wait until you and I get somewhere really alone." He pressed her hand against his hard cock. "And then I do believe you might owe me one."

8

THE AFTERNOON WAS settling in as Paige sat in her grand-father's living room staring at the chessboard.

Lyndon rubbed his chin, studying the pieces. Then he reached out decisively and moved a rook.

"Checkmate," he announced.

"What the...?" Paige blinked at the board and then saw he was right. "How the heck did you do that?" she demanded.

He grinned broadly. "You gave it to me when you didn't recognize the Kieseritzky gambit. You're not concentrating today."

Not concentrating? She was concentrating, all right, just not on chess. Ever since they'd gotten back from Gloria's, all she'd been able to think of was Zach—the feel of his hands, the slide of those fingers where she was hot and wet, his body pressing her back into the crate as she'd twisted against him, the smile she could feel on his lips even as he'd driven her to a muffled orgasm.

It had been incredible, shattering.

And a moment of lunacy, pure and simple. All right, several moments, actually. Several long, varied and memorable moments that made pretty much everything she'd experienced before with sex seem as boring as, well, tapioca pudding. But *still.*

"I must be nuts," she muttered to herself.

"Hmm?" Lyndon asked, stifling a yawn.

"Nothing," she said. "You look tired."

"I think I'll take a nap," he agreed. "You can entertain yourself for a while, can't you?"

"Don't worry about me," she assured him. Although he ought to worry—and plenty—with a granddaughter like her. What the hell had she been thinking? She hadn't been raised to be the kind of person who had sex in closets at parties, let alone while city officials and her grandfather—her *grandfather*—mingled outside. And the thought of it still made her weak and breathless and wet with the need for more.

Lyndon rose stiffly.

"Here, let me help you," she said immediately.

"I can make it," he said.

Paige took his arm anyway. "It's not often I get to walk around with such a handsome guy on my arm."

He patted her hand. "Have I told you how much I appreciate you being here right now and how much of a help you've been?"

"About a million times," she said and helped him settle into his easy chair. "I keep telling you, it's not a problem. I'm happy to do it."

His eyes drifted shut. "I just wish I had a little more excitement to offer you. It's got to be boring here for a young person like you."

"Trust me, Granddad, I've got all the excitement I need," she assured him.

Right next door, as a matter of fact.

And it was that thought that had her standing sometime later out at the gate that connected the two properties, holding the key to the padlock on her grandfather's side. The lock was well maintained—probably oiled monthly; Lyndon, she thought, would insist on it. She hadn't a clue how long it had been since the latch it had protected had been turned, though. Like the lock, the latch showed signs of oil, but the mechanism screeched in protest as she moved it.

She thought of all the years of playing before the gate as a child, of the times she'd pretended to insert a key and turn the latch and walk into another world. She was ready to have *someone* insert a key, all right. And when he turned her latch, she had a feeling that her whole world might rock a little on its axis.

Which was sort of an alarming thought, but it didn't have to be. After all, what could it hurt to explore? The situation had finite limits. Plenty of people had wild flings. Delaney, for instance, had them all the time. And now it was Paige's turn, as easy as that. All she had to do was walk through, knock on Zach's door and let it go from there.

She took a deep breath and swung the gate open wide.

It was like walking into some magical forest, cultivated and wild at the same time. Out of a clutch of moss where branch met trunk on a bay laurel bloomed an orchid in startling magenta. Ferns swept up in emerald-green arcs. The path had been maintained, Paige saw, flagstones still swept and smooth and cared for, presumably by Gloria's gardeners. All around her in the air was the scent of exotic blooms. The very air felt lush, as though it were infused with sex—or maybe it was just that right now the thought of sex permeated her being.

Nearby spread the bright aqua of the pool. Beyond that lay the Key West-style guesthouse, wide-porched, white-planked and surrounded by palms. And in there she'd find Zach.

In there she'd find Zach and they'd get naked and bring down the rafters.

"You looking for someone?"

Paige froze. She knew that voice. Slowly she turned.

Gloria Reed lay on a chaise at the edge of the pool, basking in the last of the afternoon sun. She wore a crimson bathing suit with a white cover-up and a broad-brimmed sun hat. Dark glasses covered her eyes.

"Uh, I'm so sorry, I was just…" She was just what? Paige thought wildly. Trespassing on the woman's property? Invading her privacy? Breaking the law? "I was looking for Zach," she offered lamely with a glance toward the guesthouse.

"You're not going to find him here. He went out to the store, to get guitar strings or something."

Paige turned beet-red, she knew it. Her entire face to the roots of her hair felt in flames. "I am so sorry to have barged in like this," she blurted. "I don't know what to say. This is so incredibly rude, I can't think—"

"It's okay," Gloria said, taking off her glasses.

"No, it's not okay," Paige said fervently. "I had no right to do this. I should have called, but I didn't have the number. I should have come to the front gate and rung the bell. I should have…" Oh, hell, she shouldn't have come at all.

"For chrissakes, girlie, stop babbling and take a load off," Gloria cut her off impatiently.

Paige blinked. "What?"

"Sit down and talk with me." She patted the nearby chaise. "Here."

"Oh, I couldn't—"

"You came through the gate. I'm sure you can do this." There was the faintest of edges in her voice. Paige had a sudden feeling that the Spanish Inquisition didn't have anything on Gloria Reed.

Slowly she nodded. "All right. Maybe for a few minutes, if I'm not bothering you."

"Good." Gloria settled back. "We can have a nice little

talk. Help yourself to some tea. I brought a glass out for Zach, but he was gone."

It was more order than offer, and Paige felt compelled to get the glass. "Would you like some more?" she offered.

"I wouldn't mind a freshen up, sure."

Paige settled on the chaise and gave a tentative smile. "The site visit seemed like a success."

"It was. Interesting how you and Zach disappeared, though."

Beet-red, Paige thought. "Oh, well, yes. I mean, no. I mean, just for a little. He took me back to show me some of your memorabilia and artwork." She cleared her throat. "Your home is beautiful."

"Thank you. Not a tassel or a red velvet swag in sight."

"I don't think anyone was expecting that."

"Oh, I think maybe a few were." Gloria raised her glass and took a long sip of tea through a straw, white against her carmine lips.

"Your collection is wonderful. And Zach tells me you knew Kerouac and Ginsberg?"

"We were all in San Francisco. They liked to drink and carouse, and I had a place they could do it without being bothered."

"What were they like?"

"Smart. Sarcastic. Ginsberg didn't tolerate fools, but then, I never have either. I don't get the impression you're one."

"I have my moments," Paige muttered.

Gloria gave her a steady look. Minutes ticked by and finally she nodded. "Not when it matters, I don't think," she said briskly and took a long drink of her tea.

Paige leaned forward. "Can I ask you a question?"

"Sure, ask away."

"How did you get into the whole burlesque thing?"

Gloria leaned her head back and gave that rich belly laugh. "Boy, you do jump into the deep end."

"I wasn't trying to pry. I'm sorry."

"Oh, hell, it's not prying. It was all an accident, at least at first. I mean, I grew up on a farm in Indiana. I didn't know pinups or burlesque from anything and if I'd stayed there, I'd probably have wound up some farmer's wife. Not that that's a bad thing, but between you and me, I like this better." She gave an airy wave at the pool.

"So what happened?"

"Oh, what happened was that I was out picking beans in our kitchen garden one day. Mama and Daddy were gone to town. And a man stopped on the road, the handsomest man you can imagine. Looked just like Tyrone Power, if Tyrone Power had been 4-F. Said he was a photographer out trying to get pictures for a contest he wanted to enter. And he asked would I pose for him."

"What did you say?" Paige leaned forward.

"I said yes, of course. I was fifteen," she said ruefully. "What did I know?"

"You were gorgeous."

"I was, wasn't I?" Gloria agreed. "It's funny, it was so long ago it seems like somebody else. It was hot, so I was wearing shorts and a little shirt, unbuttoned down low. He had me do things like lean against the fence and sit on the water tank. Even asked me to go in the house and put on shoes and some lipstick. Then I saw a neighbor boy drive by that I had the most excruciating crush on, so I ran up and jumped on the bottom rail of the fence to wave. When the man hollered at me, I turned around to look at him, grinning like a fool, I guess, and that was the shot."

"So how did it become a pinup?"

She shook her head. "That was my first lesson in not

trusting men. That contest wasn't any contest at all. Johnny took photos for a girlie magazine. I didn't know anything about it until some of the boys who'd gone off to war wrote that I was showing up in guys' footlockers." She rolled her eyes. "Boy, did I get in hot water over that."

"It wasn't your fault."

"It was what I got for listening to any old fella who walked by," she said. "Me, I was a sucker for the good-looking ones. They could feed me any line and I'd believe it. A coupla years later, it was a guy off one of the haying crews sweet-talked his way into my pants by saying how he wanted to marry me and settle down. Next thing I know, I'm in trouble and he's long gone." A breeze brushed over their faces, rattling the eucalyptus leaves. "Daddy and the farm were long gone by then, too, so it was just me and Mama, trying to figure out how we were going to feed ourselves and a little old baby."

"I'd have been scared to death."

"I couldn't afford to be," Gloria said frankly.

"So you went to burlesque?"

"Sort of. See, Johnny might have lied to me, but he did have one decent bone in his body. A couple of months before I got knocked up, he'd sent me a check. For the pinup," she elaborated. "It wasn't but a pittance compared to how much that picture made, but that was more than a lot of those guys did back then, let me tell you." She shrugged. "I figured I'd see if I could track him down, maybe do another. I got a couple of pictures made of me all dolled up—I've always been lucky about my figure, even after having a baby—and I sent them along. And he helped me get started."

She looked at Paige a little defiantly. "You know, a lot of people have said I lived off my body, but I've never regretted a thing I've done. I started off at seventeen without even a high school diploma, and by the time I was thirty-two I owned my own place in San Francisco. I gave my little girl a home and sent her to a good college. Whatever this narrow-minded neighborhood thinks, I'm proud of my life."

"You should be," Paige said quietly.

"All those neighbors in here today, staring and pointing fingers. I know you love your grandfather, but this museum is going to do some good, and I'm not going to let them stop me."

"I don't know how much he was concentrating on the museum," Paige confessed. "I think he was mostly just looking at the house."

"Nosy, huh? The whole pack of them are."

"He's got a reason. He grew up here."

Now it was Gloria's turn to blink. "*Here* here?"

Paige nodded. "All this, the whole bluff area, belonged to his family when he was a kid. They lost it in the Depression, except for the mother-in-law's house."

Gloria looked over at the back face of the mansion, at the spread of white stone and glass gleaming in the afternoon sun. "So all these years he's been living next door, looking over the fence." She nodded to herself. "Explains a lot."

"I think it meant something to him to see the house again and to see what a lovely job you've done with it. And the koi pond—his mother built that. He played in it when he was little."

"Hard to imagine that stiff-necked old coot as a little boy," Gloria murmured, but her eyes softened. "I guess maybe I can see why he's so upset about the museum."

"The museum's not strippers, though," Paige said. "It's something completely different. Zach showed me. If they knew, it would make a difference."

"They can pay admission when it opens."

"*If* it opens. You've still got to get it past the planning commission," Paige reminded her. "And if enough people complain, that won't happen. Why don't you try to bring them onto your side?"

"I gave up trying to cozy up to people a long time ago," Gloria retorted. "Anyway, we just had the site visit. They should have been able to see all they needed to."

"Yeah, but all you showed us was the site. You didn't show what you're planning to exhibit or why. Let them see and they'll change their minds."

Gloria shoved her glasses back on. "I shouldn't have to convince them, the narrow-minded idiots. I've known people like them my whole working life. It's none of their business what I want to do, but they'll have an opinion, sister, oh, they'll have an opinion."

"But you live in a community and that means you need to work to be a part of it. It *is* going to impact their lives, whatever you might think. So bring them over to your side."

"And how do I do that?"

"I don't know, have an open house. Promise to donate a portion of the museum proceeds to some neighborhood beautification project. You can do it. It'll work."

"What'll work?"

They both looked up to see Zach.

Pavlov's dog, Paige thought, had nothing on her. Long and lean, strong and sexy. Just the sight of him had her mouth watering. He was back in casual clothes, arms brown and sinewy and strong.

"Hey." He walked directly up and fastened his mouth over hers for a long, lingering kiss. And the heat that had gone down to low simmer while she'd been talking with Gloria bubbled up again.

bulls work—we used to see plenty of their kind when I was touring the burlesque circuit, all of them looking like they had poles up their—"

"They're not bad people, Gloria," Paige interrupted gently. "They're just scared of what they don't know and thinking the worst."

"She's right." Zach leaned back on his hands, the one closest to Paige touching her. "You want this museum. If this is a way to make it happen, then do it. It's as simple as that. Forget about soliciting their opinions—you'll only wind up ticking someone off when you don't take their advice. But the rest, yeah. It's solid."

Gloria drew her sunglasses down her nose and looked at him. "You really think it'll work?"

"It can only help. You've got the planning board on your side, but they've got to listen to the community. You don't want a roomful of people shouting about you at that meeting. If this is a way to calm at least some of them down, why not? Besides, you play it right, it'll get you a little publicity."

She pushed her glasses back up. "I'll think about it."

"You don't have long," Zach reminded her. "The planning commission hearing is in—what?—a week and a half? If you're going to do this, do it right. Have at least one room set up for real."

"_____ __ ___ ___ got? That means painting, framing, _____ __ _____ ook her head helplessly. "I couldn't _____ _ _____ igner in time. I wouldn't even know

_____ _____ spoke up. "It's what I do," she ex-_____ both stared at her. "Interior design. _____ some decisions pretty quick, but I'm _____ people to paint and frame and move furniture. And what's left over, Zach and I can do. Right?" She turned to him expectantly.

Only to find him staring at her with that same mix of humor and heat she'd come to know. "Whatever you say, chief." He caught at her hand and rose. "How about we get to work on that planning right now?"

THE DOOR TO THE guesthouse closed behind them, and just for a moment Zach dragged Paige against him, let himself feast on her mouth. Hours. He'd been aching for her for hours, since he'd stood in that closet and listened to her helpless gasps as she'd quaked against him. Ever since he'd felt her, impossibly hot, impossibly wet and so paradoxically out of reach he could only pleasure her.

He slid his hand under her shirt and Paige leaned back from him. "Wait a minute. We're not going to have sex with your grandmother sitting out there."

"Gloria? She could probably show us a thing or two."

"Really, Zach." She batted his hands away. "I mean it."

"I bet I can change your mind," he said wickedly, noticing out of the corner of his eye that Gloria had already started back to the house.

"Just wait a little while."

"But I don't want to wait," he murmured against her neck, licking his way down her throat. "And I bet I can make it so you don't want to wait, either." The skin was so soft there, fragile enough for him to feel her pulse beat against his lips. Then he dropped his head lower, onto the soft cotton of her little shirt, over the rise of her breast. He could feel the hard pebble of her nipple against his lips and he began to suck, his tongue wetting the fabric until he heard Paige catch her breath.

When she did, he slipped his hands up under the cloth.

He didn't want to make love to her by the rules, with her reserve in place. He wanted her wild and wanton, twisting against him, making noises she wasn't even aware of.

Her hands were sliding around his neck and up into his hair, down inside the collar of his T-shirt. When he felt her begin to tug at the fabric, he smiled to himself. Desire, he thought. Initiative. It was a start. It was probably something she'd done with many of her lovers. He wanted more from her than that, though. Much more.

He bit at her nipple lightly through the thin cloth and was rewarded with a strangled moan. "Oh, you're not in the closet anymore. You don't have to be quiet now."

But she did, Paige thought feverishly, even as she closed her eyes to better concentrate on the sensation. No way was she going to make noise with Gloria outside the open windows, no matter how good that hot, wet tease of his mouth was against her nipple. But it was maddening, to feel and yet not feel, to have the barrier of cloth there. She made a little growl of impatience, pulling at his shirt without thinking.

"Yep, I think we're done with this," Zach agreed, moving back enough to drag Paige's shirt off over her head and then sending his own after it.

His hands were warm and broad and she shivered as they stroked down her back, up her sides, pulling her to him so that she felt the heat of his bare torso against her own. After all the moments with clothing in the way, it seemed outrageously, extravagantly sensual. His back was smooth under her fingers, rounded with springy muscle.

And his mouth, she couldn't get enough of it, of the warm slide of his tongue over her throat, flicking at the shallow hollow at its base. With his hands loosely curled, he molded the shape of her arms, then slid his fingers up over her shoulders, drawing them along her collar bones and down over her chest, along the shallow dip of her cleavage. It made her infinitely aware of her own body, as though she were feeling it for the first time.

And she reached out to touch him, to learn the lines and dips of that tough, hard body, the solid spheres of muscle on his shoulders, the corrugations of his abs. There was something hypnotic about the smooth skin, the dusting of hair, the sheer maleness of him. The feel of his skin against her palms was a luxury and she savored it, savored knowing that he was feeling her caress.

Her hands dropped to the swell of denim at his crotch, stroking the fabric and chuckling low in her throat when she heard him suck in a breath. "I'm sorry, is that bothering you, Zach? Do you want me to stop?" she asked, reaching for his belt.

"I'll show you what I want." He shifted and with a snick, unfastened the front clasp of her bra, peeling back the cups. She felt the cool air of the room against her nipples.

And in the next instant, the heat of his mouth.

The feel of his lips and tongue kissing and licking the tender flesh had the hair prickling on the back of her neck. He nibbled and explored, tracing circles around her areola, first one, then the other, always coming closer and closer to where she was eager for his touch, drawing it out until she was making a noise of impatience. Then he fastened his mouth on a nipple.

Lust slammed through her.

This wasn't anything so pretty as desire, it was raw and primitive, driven by the heat and suction of his mouth. Gone now was the teasing. His touch was direct, dragging a response from her. With his lips he worked on one nipple, drawing it into his mouth, sucking on it, flicking it with his tongue. With wet fingers, he circled the other nipple, squeezing it, flicking it, tracing over the top until she gave a helpless groan.

And oh, when his hands moved down lower, to unbutton her shorts and let them fall, she was afraid that she would as well, so she clutched his shoulders just to keep her balance.

But Zach knelt on the ground before her and cradled her against him, arms around her waist, inhaling her, kissing her, licking his way under the sheer white panties she wore. She was quivering, she knew it, anticipation stringing her tight as a wire. She didn't gave a damn about noise anymore or who might be around. All she could do was experience the sensations rocketing through her.

Zach traced his fingertips along the legholes of the white lace she wore, down to where her thighs drew together, down to where she ached to be touched. Then he traced them back up to her hips, hooking them in the sides of the lace and drawing it down her legs in a rush, and she was naked before him.

He looked up at her, on his knees, then he wrapped his arms around her waist, pulling her against him to trace his tongue over her abdomen.

"Do you want to know what I really wanted to do to you in that closet?" he muttered feverishly, nibbling at her thighs, working his way up in between. "I wanted to do this," he said, pressing a kiss on the soft triangle at the apex. "And this." He parted her legs, with his hands, tracing the tip of his tongue over the glimmers of moisture at the edges of her hidden lips, now exposed completely to his gaze. "And this," he said and pressed his mouth to her.

And the startling heat of his tongue was on her where she was most sensitive, where she was wet and swollen and aroused.

It dragged a cry from her, sent her body jolting in shock. He parted those lips to expose her, flicked his tongue over her clit, quick and sudden, teasing and tormenting. It was gone each time before she'd even registered the touch, until she moaned in impatience, widening her stance. And then he pulled her to him hard, and put his open mouth on her. Now he swirled and stroked, tracing patterns over the sensitive flesh, licking that slick crevice. His hand slid up her thigh and one, two, three fingers slipped inside her. And when she thought she couldn't bear any more, he drew her clit into his mouth and began to suck.

Her body bucked against him.

She'd had men go down on her before, but never like this, never this hot, searing, relentless sensory assault. Never with the licking, stroking, sucking, the surprising scrape of teeth, the fingers filling her until she had to clutch at his hair to keep her feet because the tension that had filled her all day was growing, swelling, building into an orgasm that threatened to overwhelm her.

It was as though her entire body was focused on the hard little bud of her clit, the tension all tightening down, becoming more intense with each slick caress until she was shuddering, hips pumping at every touch, until every nerve of her body was wound tight with waiting. Then it slammed through her. She didn't recognize the cry it tore from her throat as she shook and quivered against Zach even as he continued his assault, every stroke of tongue sending her higher until she broke again with a long wail, shuddering and keening at the pleasure exploding through her body.

Was there anything remotely as hot as seeing calm, cool, collected Paige now, her hands trembling, eyes unfocused and mouth slack with pleasure? Zach lurched to his feet to drag off his jeans, trying not to touch himself because he was so hard even the brush of denim might take him too far. He caught her against him as she swayed, kissing her hard, openmouthed, searching for the flavors of her, feeling those strokes that only teased him with the promise of what she'd do, what they'd both do.

He'd promised to make her crazy, but he was the one going nuts. And he was dragging her down to the soft, thick carpet because the bedroom was just too damned far, his jaw clenched with the effort of holding back. He wanted to bury himself in her, deeply enough to find oblivion, but not before he'd made her come again.

And he knew he could do it, because she was already quivering at his touch, reaching to help him sheath his granite- hard cock. When she would have stroked, he had to still her hands. He had to be in her, all the way in her wet heat. The feel of her legs rising around him to wrap around his waist had him grinding his teeth. And then he was sliding into her in a hot, wet rush that almost made him explode.

Paige cried out raggedly as Zach's cock filled her. For a breathless instant, he remained poised there as they both absorbed the sensation. And then he began to stroke her. She could feel every inch of him as he moved, could feel the tip of him deep inside her, bringing himself home each time. Each time he slid into her, she saw his jaw tighten. With each stroke, she felt her arousal grow.

And it was as though he knew her body better than she did herself, because the orgasm she'd thought was over built afresh with every fractional shift of his body, of that hard cock embedded in her. Her fingertips clutched at his back, slipping on the sweat-slick ridges of muscle as she raised her hips to meet his. And he drove himself into her hot and hard, getting thicker and harder with each motion, bringing her closer and closer.

Then she was crying out with each slide, each stroke that pushed her closer and closer to a peak she'd never known and flung her, crying out, over some invisible edge. And the bursts of white-hot sensation rushed through her to the very ends of her fingertips.

THE SETTING SUN SENT golden beams across the carpet as Paige sat on the couch buckling on her sandals. She was dressed, her hair was combed, but she wasn't sure she was ever going to be quite the same again. Next to the couch an electric guitar sat in its holder. A simple instrument, but Zach could draw amazing sounds from it.

She grinned. Then again, he'd drawn some pretty amazing sounds from her, too. She'd always been fairly quiet in bed, a few moans and gasps, nothing more. She hadn't recognized the cries he'd torn from her. Then again, she'd been so far outside of her head at the time she hadn't been thinking, she'd been reacting.

She kind of liked it.

Paige reached out and strummed the strings with her fingers. Behind her she heard Zach walk up. Then he was there, his hands on her shoulders, lips pressed to the exact point where her shoulder and the nape of her neck met.

How could it take so little? she wondered as she turned her head to kiss him. She had only to catch a whiff of his deodorant, to hear him breathe, and she was hot and wet and ready.

Then he broke away and came around the couch to sit next to her. "You planning on taking up guitar?"

She nodded at the silky caramel-colored wood. "This isn't the one you played onstage the other night, is it?"

He laughed. "No, this guitar doesn't get out much."

"Why, you don't like it?"

"Don't want it to get banged up or stolen. It's an old Les Paul."

"What's that?"

"One of the first electric guitars. Gloria gave it to me when I was just a kid."

Paige ran her fingers over the glossy wood. "You've taken good care of it."

"I'd be a fool not to. It's one of the best guitars ever made. Put your feet up, I'll play you something."

"I have to get home and help with dinner for my grandfather," she said regretfully.

"I was hoping you could stay. We're not nearly done yet."

"Sorry, Granddad, I know you're starving but I have to have more sex with Zach?" She gave him a brief peck. "I don't think he'd understand us hooking up. I should get back. Maybe I can sneak out later tonight, after he goes to bed."

Zach frowned. "Didn't you stop doing that kind of thing when you moved away from home?"

"This is a different situation. You ask me, Gloria didn't seem all that thrilled about you and me either." Paige rose and headed for the door.

"But she also knows it's none of her business." He followed her.

"And I'm sure Lyndon would feel the same way."

"Are you kidding? He was trying to get you hooked up with a guy fifteen years older than you today."

"You're missing the point. All I'm saying is I'd just like to keep this low-key for now. I mean, it's not as though we're talking about anything serious anyway, right?" she asked, priding herself on how matter-of-fact she sounded.

Zach shook his head. "I think you're too serious in general. And in case it hasn't gotten through to you yet, it's my mission to get you to stop that. So the only serious we're going to talk about right now is serious fun." He pressed a kiss on her. "You cool with that?"

A vacation fling, that was all. She placed her hands on his chest and smiled up at him. "Yeah, I'm cool."

"No you're not, not yet." He slid his hands around her hips and kissed her softly. "But you've got potential." He kissed her harder. "Yeah, I'd say you've got a lot of potential."

9

LYNDON LOOKED UP FROM the paper. "Another letter to the editor about the museum," he said cheerfully. "So far, we're running three to two against. Except for this joker." He thumped the page. "Minimal traffic impact, my eye."

"Her briefing packet says she's planning to require reservations for parking," Paige said. "No reservation, no entry." She took a drink of her orange juice.

"We'll still get traffic."

"It really shouldn't be that bad."

Lyndon lowered the paper and frowned at her. "Whose side are you on, anyway?"

"I don't think it's a matter of sides."

"What's that supposed to mean?"

Paige let out a breath and carefully set the glass down in the ring of condensation on the place mat. "I need to tell you something, Granddad, but I want you to hear me out. I've taken on a new client here in Santa Barbara. There's less to do for you, and I need to keep busy." She hesitated. "I'm doing some work for Gloria Reed."

"*Gloria Reed?*" Her grandfather's brows drew down. "What could you possibly want to do with Gloria Reed?"

And that was the hard answer. "I'm helping her set up a couple of rooms as example museum exhibits so that you and the rest of the neighborhood can see what she's trying to do."

"You're helping her?" he asked incredulously. "You *know* how strongly I oppose that museum."

He saw it as betrayal, as she'd known he would. And yet... "The thing is, Granddad, I don't think you'd feel that way if you had all the information. I think when you know what she's really doing, you'll look at it differently."

"I know what she's doing," he said hotly. "Setting up a strippers' hall of fame that will draw in all sorts of riffraff, just like that tourist trap she ran in San Francisco. It had a giant painted woman straddling the front door. You walked in between her legs."

Paige stared. "*You* did?"

"Of course not," he retorted. "You know what I meant. That woman has no class."

"I think it's a question of how you define *classy*," Paige countered. "But it's not just that. She's doing this for the right reasons."

He snorted. "To make money."

"No! To help people. She's not taking a dime from the museum if it goes through. She's already got a charitable trust set up."

"She tell you that?"

"She didn't have to. She signed the contract with me in the name of the corporation. I looked it up."

There was more than anger in his eyes, Paige saw with regret. There was hurt. "So you're really determined to do this."

She squared her shoulders. "I'm going to do it because I think it's the right thing. That's what you taught me. A lot of people who worked in burlesque walked away with nothing, no big paychecks, no retirement, no benefits. Most of them don't have anything now."

"A bunch of retired strippers." His voice was dismissive.

"A bunch of retired comics and stagehands and musicians and chorus girls," she shot back. "And yes, dancers. But, my God, Granddad, they were innocent practically. You see worse today in any music video."

"Let's not talk about your modern entertainment."

"No, let's talk about helping people," she retorted. "Isn't that what you always taught me to do?"

"I taught you public service. You went into design."

The sting of it stopped her for a moment. "I'm going to ignore that because I don't think you mean it," she said slowly. "I work in design because it's what I love, but I still do charitable work and I admire the people who do more."

"You could do more if you wanted to. You're brighter than most of these monkeys in office."

"But I don't want to, not that way. And I don't think I have to. It's not just about the big-picture power brokering. Sometimes it's enough to help one person at a time." She let out a breath and took his hands. "I know this is hard for you, Granddad, but just let me do this. Come to the open house, listen to her plans. If you still think she's wrong after everything you see, then I'll work with you any way I can."

He raised his jaw and pulled his hands away. "Go do what you like," he said. "It sounds like you're going to anyway."

IF SOMEONE OFFERED him quadruple pay to do a last-minute gig, Zach thought, he'd be there in a heartbeat. Unfortunately it didn't seem to work that way for painters. No one, it seemed, could manage to break loose. So it was that he was standing in his oldest T-shirt and jeans, using a roller to swipe purple paint on the pale wall.

"I thought museums and galleries usually have white walls," he said, setting aside his roller to refill the paint tray. "Why not leave them and save the hassle?"

"Because we're not showing Jackson Pollock, that's why," Paige responded. "Anyway, these walls are cream, not white."

"Cream, white, same difference."

"Don't go into interior design," she suggested, patting his cheek. "Anyway, it's a burlesque museum. We need something a little more dramatic. Intense without being tacky."

"And purple does that for you?"

"Eggplant. And, yes, it does."

"You women and your color thing," he muttered, searching out the key to open the can of paint.

Paige straightened up from where she'd bent over the paint tray. "We women?"

"Yeah. You've always got a million names for colors. Why not call them what they are? You only do it to be confusing. Gloria's the same way."

"There, there, dear," she said gently, patting him on the back. "I'll get you a codebook."

It was the flicker of mischief in her eyes that clued him in. That and the smudge of purple—eggplant—on her chin. Pulling at the fabric behind him, he turned his head as far as it would go and caught a glimpse of a purple hand in the middle of the back of his shirt.

"You're bad," he said. "I liked this shirt."

"It has a hole on the shoulder. Anyway, you're painting. You knew it was going to get messed up."

"I was thinking artistic splatters, not a handprint," he said, rising. "What you did was messing with intent."

"It is artistic." Paige retreated, laughing, one hand purple up to the wrist.

"Nobody ever taught you to plan your commando missions, did they?" he inquired, leaning down to pick up a wet paintbrush before circling around toward her.

"Now come on, I was just being silly," she said hastily. "These are brand-new overalls. I don't want to get them all sloppy."

"They're painters' overalls. They're supposed to get all sloppy."

She made a move for the roller, but he raised the brush. "Go ahead," he invited. "Bend down."

"Retaliation is immature," she reminded him, feinting for the door but backing off when he blocked her way.

"So is slapping paint on a man when he's not looking. Good thing I didn't wear my lucky shirt." He continued moving toward her, always circling with slow-measured steps.

"Let me guess," she hazarded. "It's a white T-shirt."

"Now you're getting mean," he said, heading her off from the paint can, always working her back.

When she hit the wall behind her, she jumped. And then she understood that he'd boxed her in. Backed neatly into an unpainted corner, her only avenue of escape was to go through him and his paintbrush, which was where he intended to exact revenge.

She brandished her hand. "I've got a loaded weapon and I'm not afraid to use it."

"Neither am I," he said and pounced.

She pushed against him, and he looked down to see a purple handprint on the front of his T-shirt. "Ha-ha, you match," she crowed.

There were times a man had to get dangerous. He leaned in again and the hand with the brush moved swiftly over her cheeks. "Now you do, too," he said. "War paint."

"Why, you..." Paige stroked a finger through the paint on her cheek and streaked a line down his nose. "It's so you," she laughed.

He narrowed his eyes and tapped the brush on the tip of her nose and chin. "Oh, yeah? Try this."

Her mouth opened in outrage. And then she closed it. He saw when she changed her mind, was prepared to some extent when she flowed up against him, winding her arms around his neck. "Make love, not war," she murmured.

The kiss was hot and hard and greedy, and Zach lost long minutes to the feel of her body pressed against him. It wasn't until he registered the fact that she kept changing the angle of the kiss that he understood what she was doing.

When he moved away, he touched his fingers to his cheek. "Purple?"

"Eggplant," she said, wrinkling her nose at him.

"Perfect."

"It's a look."

"I'm sure."

"Of course," she said thoughtfully, running a suggestive fingertip down the front of his shirt, "we should go wash this off before it dries. Know any showers nearby that we could use?"

And he dropped the brush to the tarps at their feet, dragging her against him. "You know, I think this just might be my lucky shirt after all."

"Take a look at these."

Zach looked up and blinked as Gloria tossed a pair of fabric swatches in his lap where he sat on the porch glider of the guesthouse. "What about them?"

"Paige dropped them by. She says I have to pick one I like by tomorrow because you're going to L.A. to get furniture. And she says she's bringing up some pieces from her home? Do you know about this? What is she thinking?"

"Paige has some pretty strong opinions about what she likes and doesn't like. My advice is go with her judgment."

He held up the two pieces of fabric and shrugged. "Which one do you like?" He wasn't even going to ask the colors.

"I don't know. I mean, they're both nice, but they're a lot more classy-looking than I'd figured on." She dropped down to sit next to him. "I'd always sort of imagined setting up the rooms like one of the old theaters. You know, lots of dark red velvet and fancy gold leaf?"

"Works for me. Did you talk to Paige about it?"

Gloria nodded. "I think she's going for a different look. She said maybe eventually we could go that way, but right now we need to go with something a little more hoity-toity."

"Hoity-toity?" Zach raised a brow. "She said it that way?"

Gloria swatted him. "Fresh. Of course she didn't."

"If I were you, I'd listen to her. She knows how these people think. If anyone can get into their heads, she can."

"That's because she's one of them."

"Yeah?" Zach eyed her, knowing she wasn't talking about decor anymore.

"I'm just saying."

"I'm thirty-six, Gloria."

"I know."

"I've been on the road longer than I've been off it."

"I *know.*"

"Don't worry about me."

She gave him a mulish look. "It's not you I'm worried about, it's that granddaddy of hers when he finds out. You'll be lucky if he doesn't come over here hunting you down with a shotgun—and I don't mean to get you to the altar."

Zach's lips twitched. "Lyndon wouldn't do it. He'd send his gardener."

"Yeah, well, I've seen him get after the squirrels a time or two. He's not such a bad shot himself."

"I'll be okay, Gloria."

"I never said you wouldn't."

"This is just for fun."

"Am I trying to tell you what to do?"

Zach rose and tweaked her nose. "You're cute when you get all maternal."

"I'm not maternal," she growled.

"Yeah, you're just the best."

10

THE PACIFIC DESIGN Center complex in Los Angeles looked very much as if an impatient toddler had thrown down his blocks and stomped away. Zach had never seen buildings like these that looked as though they were made of crayon-colored glass. A faceted green cube nestled up to an enormous blue thing shaped like who knew what.

Stores, he discovered. Four levels of them.

"You didn't tell me this was about shopping," he muttered as they rode the escalator up.

"I told you I needed to look at a couple of pieces some of my contacts are holding for me."

"Yeah, but I thought that meant warehouses, not a mall." He looked around the glass storefronts darkly.

"We're here to help Gloria."

"Who now owes me big-time," he said.

They had shops for every damned thing, he discovered—tile, carpet, curtains, lighting, furniture, wallpaper, bathroom faucets and ceilings, not to mention the proverbial kitchen sink. Entire stores that specialized in cabinet knobs, for chris-sakes, or little gizmos that seemed to have no purpose at all.

"Accent pieces," Paige said when he held one up.

He'd seen that kind of thing at Gloria's, certainly, and God knew his mother's business depended on people buying things like that. As for him, if it wasn't musical or sound equipment and didn't fit in his van, it mostly didn't fit in his life. When you didn't have a roosting spot, you tended not to accumulate things. That had always been fine with him—his life was full enough with the distractions of the road.

Then again, in the nearly four weeks he'd been staying at Gloria's, he'd already seen himself create his own little stockpile: a few books and magazines, a couple of new shirts, a CD or two. And in those weeks, having a spot that was sort of his had gotten comfortable.

He'd always thought he was different. He'd always thought being a gypsy was okay. But somehow he'd sneakily come to like having a home. It was just another thing that made him feel like he didn't know himself anymore or what he wanted.

To distract himself, he studied Paige, instead. There was a bounce to her step that he'd never quite seen before, a simmering excitement in her eyes that made him think of sex. She was at work and she was in her element, making brisk, focused decisions with effervescent enthusiasm.

As they rode the escalator up to yet another floor, he studied her with a half smile on his face.

She eyed him. "What?"

"It's just kind of fun watching you tear the place up."

"I don't tear the place up."

"Yeah." He leaned in to kiss her. "You do. I've never seen anyone know so exactly what they needed—and get it. You're good at what you do. I like watching you. Very sexy."

She looked almost embarrassed, he was delighted to see. "What's sexy about it?"

"All those couches, for a start."

"Don't get any ideas, you. We're not fooling around in the back of someone's store."

And he tugged her toward him. "I always have ideas," he breathed over her lips, feeling the heat ignite, as ever. Underneath their feet, the steps of the escalator vibrated. In his hands, he could feel her tremble. "Maybe we've done enough shopping for now and we can just go to your house and test out your couch. Or your bed."

She moistened her lips. "Soon. We're almost done."

"Haven't we done enough?"

"Only one more store," she promised.

"Well, it had better be here, darlin', because we're on the top floor."

"I guess I'd better get to it, then, hadn't I?"

Draperies hung at the windows, thick and opulent. The furniture held the richness of ancient coins, all heavy cloth and satiny wood.

"Paige, *cara!*" A short, swarthy looking man walked up and kissed her on both cheeks. "Where have you been? I am desolate without you."

She stood back and looked him over. "I'm sure Scott keeps you from being too desolate."

"Oh, Scott is on a buying trip to Firenze so I am alone. Anyway, I do not bloom as you do," he said in his accented English. "That Santa Barbara, she agrees with you. Perhaps she will agree with me, too?"

"What would L.A. do without you?" Paige asked.

"But of course, I could not desolate my clients here. Perhaps a visit only." He glanced at Zach, beside her, and perked up. "And who's this?"

"The client's grandson."

An appreciative light came into Paolo's eyes as he looked Zach over. "And would he like a tour? We have special tours for the right sort of client," he offered.

Zach's lips twitched.

Paige tucked her tongue in her cheek. "I think he might be the wrong sort of client, Paolo. I believe Zach's the sort of client who likes his tours from me."

Paolo gave a philosophical shrug. "Then I shall leave you in the hands of the very efficient Miss Favreau, who is, I think, here to look at some seating?"

And Zach stood back and watched as she inspected first one padded bench, then another. "Copper and purple walls?" he asked.

"Eggplant," she corrected, wrinkling her nose at him. "And yes, it's going to look ravishing."

"You were right about the eggplant," he agreed. "How do you know?"

She shrugged. "Some of it's color theory. Sometimes it's a gut thing. It's like your guitar, maybe. Do you think about it when you're soloing or do you just know what works?"

"I don't know. It just…comes."

"That's kind of how this is. I can't be an artist, but I can be creative like this."

"Don't listen to her," Paolo said, stepping up briskly with forms. "She is an artist, this one. She has the purest instincts of any designer I know. Paige, *cara,* the papers for you to sign."

Paige wrote her signature with a flourish, cheeks flushed with pleasure. "Thank you, Paolo."

"I hope you appreciate you just bought my two floor models. For this sacrifice, you owe me lunch when you return, and you must bring your very handsome gentleman friend."

"My very handsome gentleman friend," she repeated, giving Zach an amused glance. "He is handsome, isn't he?"

"You have fine taste in all things, *cara,*" Paolo agreed. "Such a shame he prefers only your sort of tour."

"And he might need one right now," Zach said under his

breath as they walked out. "You 'ave me so curious about these tour, *cara*," he added, giving her a surreptitious squeeze on the behind.

Paige turned and pressed a hand against his chest. "We are done with the design center." She walked him backward until he was up against a nearby wall and leaned in to lick at his lips. When he moved to kiss her, she evaded him. "We are now on to a tour of my condo," she nipped his lower lip, "a tour of my bedroom," she caught his earlobe between her teeth, "and a tour of my bed. Interested?"

The heat and promise stunned him; the need was immediate. "Interested, but I don't think I want to wait for your condo," he said. "I've already been waiting too long."

Paige frowned as Zach headed down the broad aisle between the top floor shops. "The elevator is back behind us," she said.

"That's not what I'm looking for," he said.

The door was tucked away, innocuous. Emergency exit, it read. He didn't press the crash bar but just pushed it open. No alarm sounded; behind it were stairs going down—and up.

"Feeling in need of exercise?" She followed him inside, now frankly curious. In a flash, he pulled her to him for a molten hot kiss, releasing her while she was still reeling.

"Fresh air," he told her, and took the stairs heading upward.

"Zach, what are you doing?" she demanded. "You can't go there."

But he already had the door open to reveal the sun. "Come on. The water's fine."

It was smaller than she'd expected, the door leading into a living-room-sized well sunk into the surrounding blue of the building. The walls were faced in painted aluminum;

the square shapes of vents and air-conditioning equipment poked out of the gravel surface at intervals.

"You're insane," she informed Zach as she walked outside. "If you wanted to be outdoors, why didn't you tell me? There's an observation deck on three. We could have had lunch."

And in a flash he'd pulled her to him for another of those hot, mind-melting kisses. "We can do more than have lunch up here," he breathed against her lips. He ran his hands down over her body, palms hard, proprietary. "Lots more."

Like a stored-up charge jumps a gap, so heat snapped between them, flashing throughout her entire body, sending every neuron to instant alert.

She'd ridden a roller coaster at Disneyland once, sat in the cars waiting for the traditional long, slow ratchet up the high hill. Instead, in the blink of an eye, the train had gone surging forward, snatching the air from her lungs, and in the subsequent minutes she never got it back.

She felt like that now, paralyzed with desire, unable to think, nearly unable to breathe save in gasps. Where the sudden hunger had come from, she couldn't say, only that with Zach it was never far away. Where she'd gotten the daring not to care about propriety but only about pleasure was easier—that was him and only him.

His mouth was hot, his hands demanding as they smoothed down over her body, sliding up the sides of her thighs and bringing her skirt up with them. She could feel him hard against her and the knowledge made her giddy, sent need slamming through her.

"You're so sexy, so hot," he muttered feverishly in her ear. "I want to be inside you. I want to fuck you out here until we both come."

It thrilled, it alarmed her. Most of all, it turned

"Come on," she murmured. "Now." She reached out for his zipper. When she drew him out, hot and pulsing in her hand, it intoxicated her. She knew how wet she was—he'd slipped two fingers underneath her lacy thong to stroke her clit, each touch sending that buzz through her that made her helpless to do anything but want. Then he hooked the scrap of cloth out of the way and with a movement of his hips, impaled her with a suddenness that had them both groaning.

It wasn't about finesse. It was nothing so sophisticated as seduction. It was about intoxication and chance, all hard and fast and relentless, and all the more arousing for it. Zach dragged her legs up around his waist and drove himself up and into her so hard on each thrust that she was right on the line between pleasure and pain. Pressing her open mouth on his, inhaling him as she felt him harden and thicken, she felt her own orgasm billowing up, faster than it had ever happened for her before. She moved her head to stare down at the frankly riveting sight of their joined bodies, his cock moving in and out of her.

And then she was coming, shaking and quivering against him, crying out even as he still drove her a few more strokes to his own climax.

She'd had every intention of protesting, Paige thought hazily as they moved apart, but somehow in the heat and liquid pleasure of the moment the words went out of her head. This wasn't the kind of thing she did, going into off-limits areas, letting a man kiss her mindless. Even when the man had talented hands and a clever mouth.

n't anything that she'd ever in a million years ined doing.

 anything that she'd have given up.

Zach's astounded eyes, she threw her head noon sky and laughed.

"DO YOU EVER STUMBLE across people days after your parties are over, still trying to find their way out?" Zach asked as he walked from Paige's stylishly unfussy bedroom to her office.

Paige looked up from the catalog she'd been thumbing through and made a face at him. "You've been living at Gloria's for the last few weeks and you can even ask me that? This is a mouse hole compared to her place."

"A nicely decorated mouse hole," he observed. Half a floor in a nineteen twenties apartment building converted to condos, to be exact, and furnished with the seemingly unplanned effortlessness that he now knew cost a bundle. They'd stopped by so that the movers could pick up some of her pieces to take to Gloria's for the open house. And he walked through the rooms, savoring the ghost of her scent in the air, picking up and setting down items that were part of her life.

Some of it was art and sculpture that reflected her style, but it was the little stuff, the plastic neon crawdad sitting atop her refrigerator, the postcard of Elvis and Nixon on her bulletin board that made him smile. In a framed photograph that sat on her filing cabinet, a tiny blonde girl dressed up as Princess Leia stood beaming between her parents, holding their hands. Zach studied the smile more closely and turned to Paige. "You?"

A matching smile bloomed across her face and she crossed the room to him. "Me with my parents. I think I was four."

She'd gotten the ballerina looks from her mother, he saw, and there was a naughty little glint in both of their eyes. On the other side, Paige's father stood looking happily bemused.

"What's your mother dressed up as?"

"She was Han Solo." Paige stroked a finger over her mother's hair. "Created quite a stir. It was a kids' dress-up party, not for adults, but my mother always said some rules were made for breaking."

His mouth curved. "I think I'd have liked your mother." He slipped his arms around her waist from behind.

"I think you would have, too. She probably would have called you a good influence."

"See?" He dropped a kiss on her hair. "Smart woman. She'd have been proud of you today."

"When, working?"

"No. After. Some rules were made for breaking, right?"

Paige pirouetted on her toes and pressed her lips to his. "You're a good guide for that. Anyway, we should get going if we're going to miss traffic. We're already running late. If you wouldn't mind carrying the satchel, I can get my bag and we can go.

"What have you got in here, rocks?" he asked as they walked out to her car.

"Some reference books I need, my laser measurer, that kind of stuff. And clothes," she said, holding up the other bag.

"You don't have enough already?"

"After two weeks, I need some variety. Besides, you know how it is, there are always things you forget when you travel."

"That's why my motto is always keep it simple." He hoisted the bags into her trunk.

"Where did you learn that, traveling-musician school?" She gave him a quick kiss of thanks.

"My mom. She was pretty strict about what we could bring on the circuit."

"You had the home base in winter."

"And five people in an RV in the summer," he said as they got into the car and she started it up.

"And then, what, you moved out to live with wolves?"

She came to a halt at the end of her street before turning onto the boulevard.

Not a bad description, he thought, remembering the chaos of those years. "I crashed with some other guys at first while I was in between tours. It was always a pain in the ass, though. I hated being stuffed in with that many people for that long, so I just got to where I stayed on the road."

"And lived with that many people in a little van," she said drily. "That sounds much better."

"That was just to get from city to city. Cheap hotels, you get your own room, depending on what the gig pays." He looked up at the houses they drove past, the houses perched up on the neighboring hills. People lived in them, left them every morning and came back every night.

It was a different world.

Paige weaved her way toward the freeway down a street already clogged with cars. "Oh, hell," she said, remembering.

"What?"

"I forgot to call someone." She rummaged for her cell phone. Her hands-free cord, she thought, was in the back seat, buried under satchels and boxes and who knew what. It just meant she'd have to make it quick. At a stoplight, she hit a speed dial number and listened to the tones in her ear.

"Hello?"

"Delaney? It's Paige."

"Hey, sweet pea, how are ya?"

"Good. How 'bout yourself?"

"Can't complain. How's Santa Barbara?" In the background, Paige heard Franz Ferdinand playing.

"Actually, I'm in L.A. right now."

"You're back? Cool!"

"Just for the day," Paige cautioned. "I had to come down and get some furniture."

"Oh, my God, you're moving."

Paige laughed and circled around a large truck that was double-parked on the right. "No, I'm not moving. I'm picking some stuff up to take back. I've got a client in Santa Barbara that I'm dressing some rooms for. It's an open house for a museum and it's got to look right."

Delaney processed that. "Wait a minute—this doesn't have anything to do with the museum thing next door, does it?"

"Uh-huh."

"But wasn't your grandfather having conniptions over it?"

Paige winced a little. "Well, yeah."

"And he's changed his mind?"

"Maybe after the open house."

"So let me get this straight. You're loaning your own furniture, which you're compulsive about, to the lady next door so that she can convince people to let her put in a museum, the very idea of which gives your grandfather, whom you adore, fits." Seconds passed and then Paige heard an explosion of breath. "Oh. My. God," Delaney said in rising tones. "The musician. You're schtupping him, aren't you?"

Paige hastily turned down the volume on her phone. Next to her, Zach looked amused. "I'm sorry, but I didn't hear you."

"Oh, you are, aren't you? You've got to tell me everything," Delaney demanded. "Now."

"I'm afraid I can't right now," Paige returned smoothly, pulling to a stop at a light. "I'm driving in my car. No hands-free."

"I'll hold the phone for you," Zach offered.

Paige threw him a dirty look.

"Who was that?" Delaney demanded. "Was that him? Is he there with you in your car?"

"Yes, that's correct," Paige said, pulling forward. "Can I get back to you on that?"

"Only if later is tonight. The Supper Club's meeting and you have to stop in. With the boy toy."

"You're out of your mind," Paige told her.

"What's the problem?"

"Where do I start?"

"I'm not talking about dinner, I just meant for drinks."

"We're trying to miss traffic."

Delaney laughed. "It's already after four-thirty, sweet pea. Traffic started backing up over an hour ago. Come on, we're meeting at six. I'll text-message you directions. You guys stop in for a drink and go—you won't really get home all that much later anyway. Come on," she cajoled. "We haven't seen you in ages."

"Two weeks."

"With what you've got going on, it's like dog years," Delaney exclaimed. "Please come? Pretty, pretty, pretty, pretty please?"

Paige sighed and looked at Zach. "Do you mind stopping by to say hi to some friends of mine? We won't stay long. I usually see them every week and it's been a while."

"And here I was looking to go home and do some schtupping. This isn't going to be a chick thing, is it? Am I going to have any friends in the room?"

"Tell him Kev and Rand will be there," Delaney said. "He can go off and talk about car engines and Jessica Simpson with them."

"Jessica Simpson?" Paige echoed.

"Men are men, honey. Anyway, Trish and Ty are off on

location, and Sabrina's got a meeting with her backers. So how many is that?"

"Four women, two guys and us," Paige reported to Zach.

He considered. "Long odds, but I suppose I should show some guy solidarity. Sign me up."

"We'll be there," Paige told Delaney and ended the call.

Zach settled more comfortably in his seat. "Now, about this schtupping."

THE BAR WAS CROWDED, the decibel level loud. And Zach did his damnedest to keep up. He wasn't entirely sure he had all the names straight, but he was nodding at the right times, he thought. And he seemed to have something in common with at least one of them.

"Guitar player, huh?" Kev said, shaking his hand. "The name's familiar. I'll have to check my stacks when I get home."

"Don't be too disappointed if you don't find anything," Zach said.

"Oh, trust me, we probably do have it. The man's got an entire roomful of CDs and albums," Kelly said.

"'Zat so?" Zach eyed Kev speculatively. "Always nice to meet a music lover."

Kelly sipped her virgin margarita. "Hopefully Kev Jr. will be, too, considering that's where the nursery goes."

"Can't you just let them sleep in the bathtub for the first year?" Rand asked.

"That's how you get turned in to Child Services, dear," Cilla said, patting his cheek.

"But they're kind of small," he protested.

"Okay, remember that conversation we've been having about kids? Maybe we ought to back up and just start with a goldfish."

"They can live in the bathtub," Rand said triumphantly.

Kev, who'd been nursing his drink, suddenly snapped his fingers. *"Delta Waters,"* he burst out.

Silence fell as seven pairs of mystified eyes turned to him.

"Delta Waters?" Kelly repeated.

"The tribute album," Kev said to Zach. "That's where I know you from. You did a cover of 'I Tried Hard' by John Lee Hooker."

There was nothing like running across someone who knew his stuff, Zach thought, except being onstage in front of an audience where it clicked. "Yeah, that was me."

"Well, hell, it's nice to meet you, man. You should hear this guy," he said to the group. "Amazing guitarist, just amazing. Where you playing these days?"

Zach shrugged. "Here and there. I'm taking it slow right now."

"I've got a Strat of my own. I mostly play rhythm, though." He brightened. "Hey, you ever come to town to play, there's this guitar shop over in Santa Monica that has kind of a pickup night on Mondays. Whoever's in town shows up, even some of us amateurs. You oughta come by and play. It's no frills, just the real deal."

"What's it called?"

"McCall's. I found out about it from a buddy of mine who has a little sound studio. He records some indie bands." Kev glanced around the rest of the group. "Listen, why don't we go up to the bar and I can buy you a drink, let the girls talk about baby stuff?"

"Count me in," Rand interrupted with a hasty look at the female contingent of the Supper Club.

"You don't want to hang around for some hot girl talk, sweetie?" Cilla purred, patting his behind.

"You folks are black belts. I'm still a novice." He leaned

in and kissed her thoroughly, leaving her to settle back with a dreamy look as he walked away.

"You going to be okay, babe?" Kev asked Kelly. "I'll be right over here if you need anything."

"I don't think I'm going to go into labor in the next half hour, hon. Get out of here and leave us to it," Kelly shooed them away and went to Paige with the other women.

"My God, Paige, he's gorgeous," Delaney said. "Like eat him with a spoon."

Kelly fanned herself. "I'll say. Tell us everything," she demanded. "Who, what, when, where and how."

"Especially how," Cilla added wickedly.

Thea leaned forward. "Have you seen him onstage?"

For a moment Paige let herself remember the heat, the pure sexuality of the moment. "The man can play."

Delaney peeked under the table. "I think I just saw your thighs go up in flames."

"There's something about a man with a guitar in his hands," Kelly said dreamily.

"It's called foreplay," Delaney said. "So was that what decided you?"

"That was when I kissed him."

"Wait a minute," Cilla interrupted. "Back up. Some of us haven't even heard how you met."

"Okay. You remember I had to leave here because my grandfather was in an accident, right?"

Thea stirred. "He's okay now?"

"He is, thanks for asking. Still a little beat-up but getting around." Although none too happy with her at the moment, but that would take care of itself in time. "Anyway, he got into an accident running into his next-door neighbor, who happens to be Zach's grandmother. So Zach was in the E.R., I was in the E.R...." She shrugged.

"And what? You were locking lips over the gauze?" Kelly said skeptically.

"Are you kidding? I thought he was a biker or something," Paige said. "He kind of scared me."

Delaney took a drink of her Cosmopolitan. "That's part of the fun, isn't it?"

"So your grandfather got into a car accident just to set you up with the boy next door?" Cilla's eyes twinkled with mischief.

"Hardly."

"You know how much grandparents like to get their little chicks settled."

Paige snorted. "I think my grandfather would commit hara-kiri before setting me up with Zach. He and Zach's grandmother have a permanent feud going."

"A feud?" Thea folded her arms on the table and leaned forward. "Now this is starting to get interesting."

"That's one way to describe it," Paige said, poking at the ice in her tea with a straw.

"Do they know?"

"About Zach and I? His grandmother does."

"Haven't had the nerve to tell Grandpa yet?" Thea sympathized. "What do they do, burn down each others' barns?"

"Call the city on each other mostly and cut down one another's plants."

Kelly grinned. "Urban warfare."

"While their grandchildren are sneaking back and forth between houses. Ain't that just romantic," Cilla sighed.

"I don't know, judging by the way they look at each other, romance doesn't have much to do with it," Delaney drawled. "And is he as good as he looks?"

"I'll settle for just the highlights," Kelly put in. "I mean, please don't tell me he's one of your standard-in-the-sack missionary boys."

"Standard, he's not," Paige said, watching him laughing with Kev and Rand. "Every place and every way you can imagine." *In a closet, with a gang of people milling around outside.*

Kelly winked. "Ooh, I like the sound of that."

"Way to go Paige," Delaney said. "About time you got done good and proper. I could go kiss him for getting you to loosen up. In fact—" her eyes gleamed "—maybe I will."

"Sorry, I've got dibs," Paige told her. *For now.*

"So how much longer are you staying up there?" Thea asked as though she'd heard Paige's thoughts. "It seems like you've been gone forever."

"I don't know. Until my grandfather doesn't need me anymore. A couple of weeks, anyway."

"If going home means saying goodbye to your guy, then I'd make sure Grandpa is really, really healthy before you leave," Delaney said.

"Zach might be headed back out on the road before then anyway," Paige said and felt a little twinge at the thought. Actually, more than a twinge. A lot more. Zach mattered to her. She liked being with him. She liked who she was with him. She glanced over at him abruptly.

To find him looking straight at her.

It was like some invisible line of communication humming between them, some unseen connection. And then he glanced away at something that Kev said.

And for the first time she understood how empty life was going to be like when he was gone.

11

THE PACIFIC COAST HIGHWAY unfurled in a dark ribbon before their headlights. The cooling air held the scent of the sea. Next to them, the moon sent a glistening swath of silver light across the waves. The miles drifted by in a companionable silence that Paige felt no need to break.

Funny how time changed things. A little over two weeks before, she'd thought Zach was a biker, disreputable, the kind of man who made her a little uneasy just being in the room. Now he'd become a fixture in her days.

And nights.

And yet in many ways they were still strangers. There was so much they didn't know of each other. How, then, could she feel such an easy connection?

She reached over and squeezed his hand. "Thanks for coming with me," she said.

"What are you thanking me for? You're the one doing all the work."

"You're helping, too."

"I'm a pair of extra hands. You're the one giving up your furniture and time. If this museum thing goes through, a lot of it will be because of you."

"Gloria's done all the advance work," Paige said, watching the lights of oncoming cars strobe over the road.

"Doesn't matter. I think this thing Saturday has the possibility of tipping the balance, and that's all you."

"Don't pin your hopes on Saturday. I'm only guessing it will work. We might get lucky or we might not."

He reached over and stroked a hand up her thigh. "I think I can pretty well guarantee you're going to get lucky, darlin'," he drawled.

"Ooh, I hope so. Although maybe not until I get off this twisty patch."

He slid his fingers up higher. "Are you suggesting a little driving entertainment? Just for future reference, it works better when you wear a skirt."

"I'll keep that in mind," she said.

This time he reached out for her hand. Neither really thought about the fact that their fingers remained linked as time passed.

"So that was fun that Kev knew of you," Paige said. "I should have expected that. I'd forgotten what a blues nut he is. And knowing a guy with a recording studio… It makes sense, I suppose. He has to do sound mixing on some of the commercials he does. You ever heard of the place?"

"No, but there are a lot of indie studios out there."

"I guess it wouldn't matter to you anyway. You've already got a recording contract."

"Used to, anyway," he said.

It took her a minute to register the words. "What do you mean?"

He didn't answer right away. When she glanced over, he was staring out at the night. "My label dropped me last month," he said.

"But I don't understand," she said blankly. "You're an amazing player. I looked you up online. The critics love you."

"But I don't sell. It's a business. What counts is the numbers."

"But Kev was raving about you. How can you not sell?"

He gave a humorless laugh. "The million-dollar question. Or in my case, the three-hundred-and-forty-six-dollar question, which was my last royalty check. Anyway, the band was already breaking up when we got the news."

"Why? Personality conflicts?"

"Not really. We've been together too long for that. But some of the guys have families. The road gets to be a hard place."

"Even for you?"

He was quiet for a while. "Sometimes," he said finally. "When it does, I usually come see Gloria for a week or two. But I don't have a wife and kids looking to me to be there."

"So what are you going to do?"

He gave a short, humorless laugh. "I don't know. It's hard to get a good booking schedule without record company support. My manager's not returning calls."

Her fingers tightened in his. "Something will work out. You're too talented for it not to."

"I always figured it would. I just…"

"What?"

He shrugged. "I just wonder, sometimes, if that's enough. I've been busting my ass at this for so long." He fell silent.

"You'll find a way," she murmured. "Even if it doesn't look like it right now. You could produce your own album with Kev's friend."

"I don't have the cash for that. Besides, I'm a musician, not a record distributor. I play. That's what I do." He shook his head briskly. "Anyway, I'll work something out. I just wanted some time to chill, and one thing Gloria never is is depressing."

"Lucky for her that you happened to be around, considering what's gone on."

"Lucky for me Gloria happened to be around, more like." He squeezed her hand. "Lucky for me you happened to be around, too."

"I guess we're both lucky that way," she said.

THE WALLS OF THE exhibit rooms were painted, the furniture had arrived. It was time to hang the art and the costumes, Paige thought, looking at her to-do list. Unfortunately the fixtures for the clothing wouldn't arrive for a day—assuming all went smoothly, which it almost never did—leaving her itchy and worrying about the schedule.

She needed something to keep herself busy or she was going to go crazy. She'd checked on Lyndon so many times she was wearing a path in the grass back to the house. Running errands would help, she decided, or at least get her out of the house so it was harder to fret. She'd need hardware to hang the fixtures and card stock to label things.

Out in the hall, she heard whistling, and Zach walked into the room.

It never failed to give her that surge of anticipation, the sight of him, the sound of his voice.

"Hey, gorgeous," he said, crossing to give her a quick kiss that stretched out into more.

"Hey, yourself," Paige murmured finally.

"What are you doing?"

"Making a list."

"Checking it twice?"

She wrinkled her nose at him. "Trying to make sure we get everything done before Saturday. I'm going to pick up the hardware and check with the fixtures store."

He nodded thoughtfully. "Okay. How about if I go with you?"

"But you hate shopping."

"So. It's a nice day and we can borrow Gloria's convertible. What do you say?"

STATE STREET WAS crowded on a weekday morning, but Paige sighed in pleasure as the sun shone down on her shoulders, exposed by her sleeveless top. "It's nice to get out," she said. "It's easy to forget there's an outside world."

"Something to be said for it," Zach agreed. The light changed and they headed down the next block.

"The hardware store is right up here, on the right. You can park anywh—hey!" she yelped as he put on the gas and drove right by it. "What are you doing?" Paige demanded, staring back at the store they'd passed. "That was where we needed to go."

"Not today we don't. No shopping, no list making. Today we're playing hooky."

"Have you forgotten we've got an open house in exactly two days?"

"We're cool. You said yourself that there's not much on the to-do list."

"It doesn't happen on its own, Zach."

"And what you're doing today is make-work because you're nervous. Why not relax, do something off the cuff? You've been busting your behind for days. Take a break."

He didn't, as she'd expected, head to the beach. Instead he turned inland, onto the highway that threaded its way up into the Santa Ynez Mountains.

"Don't tell me, you've got a sudden yen for Danish pastry and you're kidnapping me to Solvang," she said. She remembered her grandparents taking her this way as a child, to visit the tiny Scandinavian tourist enclave with its windmills and wooden shoes.

Zach shrugged. "Dunno. We'll wind up where we wind up."

"You're kidnapping me and you don't even know where we're going?"

"North," he said simply. "I'll work the rest out as we go."

The road ahead began to rise. Around them loomed hillocks of yellow sandstone, the outliers of the mountains that rose sudden and sheer ahead.

She turned to glance idly at Zach as he adjusted his sunglasses. The dark lenses gleamed; stubble that he hadn't bothered to shave that morning blued his chin. He looked no less dangerous now than he had the first time she'd seen him. Only now instead of alarming her, it aroused.

They blasted out of a turn and up the mountain.

"I can't remember the last time I was up this way," Paige said aloud. "I usually just come to see Granddad."

"See? I do broaden your horizons."

"You've broadened them in a lot more ways than just taking me for a drive," she said.

Zach glanced at her. "We aim to please, ma'am."

They began threading their way up the switchbacks that led to the San Marcos Pass, now cutting between masses of solid rock, now hugging the mountainside. The two-lane road wove its way through sharp arcs, rising and doubling back on itself like spaghetti. Over the guardrails she caught glimpses of the void, of the dusty green of mesquite and the rounded sandstone boulders far below.

The mountainsides were warm gold in the sunlight. Zach drove fast and skillfully, accelerating out of the curves, passing when it was clear. Paige smelled the sharp, turpentine scent of piñon and the chaparral. Looking back, she could see the glittering blue of the Pacific.

Zach downshifted as they rose higher, following the twisting road up, always up. Now the air seemed clearer, the sky bluer. They crested the pass, driving along a short stretch of level road before they began to drop. And suddenly everything changed.

One minute they were in claustrophobic mountains, surrounded by rock. The next it was as though they'd vaulted off into space. They were on a bridge crossing a wide gorge with the broad, rolling vista of the Santa Ynez Valley opening out before them in a miniature patchwork and they could see for miles.

Paige laughed in pure exhilaration. "Zach, this is wonderful."

Beyond, the serried ranks of distant ranges framed the valley. Below, live oaks dotted rolling hills. This time of year, it was still green; by summer, she knew, they would be baked gold. She caught the glint of blue water in the distance, the brown smudges of cattle on the hillsides.

"Cool, huh?"

"Better than cool. What a view. I wish we could just stop right here."

"I think we can do something about that." Zach watched the road and made an abrupt turn to the right, into a turnout, she realized.

"You've brought me to a Lovers' Leap?" she asked, raising a brow as he parked.

"We don't have to leap," he said with a leer. "You could just jump me."

"Not right now, cowboy," she said.

He turned off the car and opened the door. "What, are you afraid of sunburn?"

Buff-colored sandstone boulders ringed the edge of the turnout; beyond, the hillside dropped away in a slope so steep that all the valley was laid out below.

"It's so gorgeous," Paige sighed. "You know, everyone assumes California is just L.A. and smog and freeways. There's so much more, but no one ever sees it except us."

"That's not necessarily a bad thing." Zach leaned against a hip-high boulder. "I mean, look at Yosemite Valley. Everyone knows about it and they have traffic jams and smog in a national park. It's kind of nice having spots like this that are sort of ours."

She gave him an impish grin. "Is this the part where you get out your pocketknife and carve our names in a boulder for all time?"

He shook his head. "Nah. Number one, I don't want to be an idiot. Number two, I don't want to leave my name showing everyone exactly which idiot I am. We'll just have to remember it some other way." He stared off into the distance, then threw up his keys and caught them. "I just figured out where we're going, though. Is our work here done?"

"That depends on what comes next."

He kissed the tip of her nose. "It's a surprise."

"A winery?" she suggested, scrambling after him.

"Wait and see."

"Alcohol is a great way to relax."

"I'll keep that in mind," he said.

Now the road looped smoothly down to the valley floor, scooting between boulders, under the branches of bay laurel and olive trees. Paige put a hand out the window, letting it fly idly in the slipstream.

"Have you ever had a motorcycle?" she asked curiously.

He gave her a puzzled look. "A motorcycle? Why, you hot for riding on the back of a hog?"

"No. You just seem like the kind of guy who would like them. Do you?"

He shrugged. "Yeah, but it's kind of hard to fit guitars and a sound system on a bike."

"I guess there's that," she said. "Does it ever bum you out, the stuff you give up to be on the road?"

He gave a humorless laugh. "Sweetheart, if I ever stacked up all the things I've given up for my music, I'd have my head examined."

And then he got onto the shoulder and turned. *Cachuma Lake, County Park* proclaimed a sign at the corner.

Paige glanced at him. "You have a bass-fishing obsession I don't know about?"

"You might say that," he said happily, handing a five to the ranger in her little kiosk.

In summer, Paige imagined, the area was crowded with RVs and boats, the air filled with the scent of burning charcoal and the shouts of children. Now, though, it was a weekday morning, too late for spring break and too early for vacationers. The area was quiet.

"We don't have the stuff to hike or swim. What are we going to do?"

"I don't know, rent a boat? Cruise the lake?" Zach popped the trunk and poked around, coming up triumphantly with a blanket. "Hard seats," he explained.

"Rent a boat," she echoed and followed him to the dock. "Do you know how to sail?"

"No sailboats," he said. "Power."

The attendant pocketed Zach's twenty and nodded to the row of aluminum motorboats bobbing at the pier. "You got your choice." The refreshment stand wasn't open yet, but they bought bottled water and candy bars and chips from a vending machine.

"See," Zach said. "A picnic."

"You've been studying that FDA food pyramid again, haven't you?"

"Sugar and grease, two of the four food groups."

The little silvery boats nudged gently against the wooden pilings of the dock. Zach nodded to them. "Which one do you like?" he asked.

Paige inspected the little craft dubiously. "You sure you know how to run one of these things?"

"Sure," he said, choosing one and starting the engine.

She stepped in the boat, wobbling a bit, and he scooped her against him, taking the opportunity to squeeze her derriere while he was at it.

"Did you just grope me?" she asked, smoothing her shorts as she sat.

"Who, me? Never." He started the engine and turned back to her. "Okay, where to?"

She closed her eyes and pointed. "That way."

And then they were speeding out over the lake, nothing but blue all around them, the wind in their hair.

12

SHE'D NEVER THOUGHT that skimming over the water in a tiny power boat would be fun. The lake was bigger than she'd ever guessed, ringed by dusty green hills that gave way to grayish and then purple-blue mountains beyond. On the map at the boathouse, the lake had reminded her of one of those dragons from the Chinese New Year parades, blocky head flowing into a sinuous trailing body to a forked tail. Long inlets branched off like legs, poking into the rock bluffs that rose on the far side.

They had the water to themselves, with the exception of a few fishermen and a pelican who flew low on great beats of its snowy white wings, trolling for lunch. It kept pace with them for a few minutes, then, without warning, it dived, smacking into the water with an explosive splash. An instant later it bobbed on the surface of the wavelets, looking annoyed.

"Guess it missed," Zach said over the growl of the engine. He brought the boat in closer to the shoreline, studying the rocks.

"What are you doing?" Paige asked.

"Looking for someplace with a beach where we can stop."

"It looks like there are some places down there," she said pointing to the far end of the lake.

"I remember seeing some inlets around here on the

map." He ran the boat along the shore, studying the terrain. Before them rose only rock bluffs, though.

And suddenly he was heading straight toward them.

"What are you doing?" Paige asked. "There's nowhere here to go." Then she blinked and then she looked again.

It was deceptive, she saw as they came closer. The shore curved around, the play of light on the sandstone and water tricking the eye so that what appeared to be a shadow was in reality a hook of rock that hid another of those protected inlets.

Zach let the boat come to idle and gave her a considering look. "Want to check it out?"

"Sure."

The inlet cut deep into the rock, she saw as they motored down into it, the sound of the engine echoing off the sandstone walls. At the far end, the bluffs fell away to reveal a small pebble-strewn beach rising into the dusty green of olive and bay laurel trees.

Zach eased the boat forward. With a faint shudder, the prow nudged into the smooth shingle that lined the shore. The water was warmer than she'd expected, Paige discovered as she stepped out into it, a combination of sun and shallow water. She clutched her sandals and the bottles, wading to dry land.

Zach fastened the boat in place and grabbed the food and the blanket. "Pick a tree, any tree," he offered as they walked up onto the beach.

Pebbles gave way to dirt and even a bit of grass under the spreading branches of a live oak near where Zach spread the blanket. From the woods nearby came the occasional rapid-fire knock of a woodpecker and the light drone of an early cicada. Out in the inlet, the water glimmered under a sky of vivid blue.

pered through her. They were out in the open, she thought, feeling the warmth of the dappled sunlight on her skin. And when he stripped off the last of her clothing, it felt as good as anything ever had.

Zach's hand curved around her breast, bringing it to his mouth for the liquid caress of his tongue. She sucked in a breath as he rubbed his lips against first one nipple, then the other. Closing her eyes, she focused only on the slick touch, the warmth, the feel of his hands on her.

Once upon a time, aeons ago it seemed, she'd watched those hands, wondered how they'd feel on her skin. Now she gasped a little as they slid over her breasts, pushing them together so that he could rub his chin over her nipples, making her jolt at the surprising bolt of pain followed by the warm wet of his tongue.

Arousal. It made her hungry for him.

It made her bold enough to take what she wanted.

She pressed against him until he raised his head. "What?"

"I think you should just roll over and relax for a while," she said, "let the lady drive."

"My pleasure," he said, a glint of amusement in his eyes.

She took her time, making a long, leisurely exploration of his body, pressing her lips against the firm, slightly rough skin of his neck, trailing her tongue over his chest to nibble on his nipples, one after the other.

Theirs had been a relationship of so much heat and urgency that she'd never had a chance to really learn his body. But here in this suspended moment that was theirs alone, she could. Now she touched and watched, experimenting with a brush here, a lick there, to see what made him quiver, what made him moan. And always, always, she dropped down toward what she craved.

Straddling his legs, she unbuckled his belt and pulled

down his zipper to free the stiff bounce of his cock. The arousal thrumming through her intensified. She swallowed, staring at it, thick and hard and flat up against his belly. "You seem to have yourself a little problem there."

"Never use the word *little* when talking about a man's equipment, darlin'."

"My mistake," she said. "Any way I can make it up to you?"

"I can think of a few."

"So can I. First, these come off." She tugged at his belt loops.

"My jeans?"

"If I have to be naked, so do you," she said firmly.

He sighed. "The things I'll do for a blow job."

She grabbed the bottom of his pant legs and pulled, sliding them off. Then she moved into place, leaning down. His cock was hard, the head purplish in the sunlight. She nuzzled it with her nose, then breathed on it, watching it bobble a bit in reaction. Wetting her fingertip, she slicked one of her nipples and then rubbed the firm nubbin over the point on the underside of his cock where she knew he was most sensitive.

She was rewarded with a groan. "Do you like that?" she asked, repeating the motion.

"You look so hot," he muttered, watching her.

She stroked him a few more times, then shifted so that she was leaning directly over him again. With the tip of her tongue she licked his hard glans and was rewarded with a shudder. Then she licked him again, from base to tip as if he were a lollipop, giving him a little flick at the tip.

His breath hissed in.

So soft, so hard, his erection pulsed. Now she caught it in her hand and held the tip up to her lips, letting just the very end slide inside, getting it good and wet, swirling her tongue around it until he was clenching fistfuls of the blanket.

And with a sudden motion of her head she slid him all the way inside.

It wrenched a groan from him.

There was nothing like this feeling, she thought, knowing he was aroused, knowing what each movement she made was doing for him. Lips wrapped around him, she slid him in and out of her mouth, her fingers ringing his shaft to keep him wet, to make him even harder. With her tongue she stroked the sensitive underside of his cock. She heard his ragged breath, savoring the immediacy, the knowledge of the pleasure that she could give him, knowing that at that moment he was focused only on those sensations.

And then she let him slip out of her mouth. Ignoring his ragged gasp of disappointment, she moved up to straddle him again, this time poising his cock at her opening. And with a pump of his hips he slid up inside her, where she was already slick and wet.

For a moment she was absolutely still, savoring the sensation. Then she began to move up and down on top of him, feeling him go deep in a new way that made her cry out, where it felt she couldn't possibly take any more but that if she stopped she would die. With every stroke she felt him all the way up inside, his hands on her hips, guiding her, setting the pace as she tightened herself around him. The struggle for control drew his features taut.

She wanted release, she wanted to be suspended in this particular moment of connection. She moved her hands to her breasts to pleasure herself, knowing what the sight would do to him. And immediately his cock got thicker and harder, as it did just before orgasm. Every time she moved, his cock stroked her clit. Every time she moved, she dragged them both closer to orgasm, every stroke tightening the pleasure down to one tiny spot, that one spot from which all sensation radiated.

The sun was warm on her shoulders and she gloried in it, in the pleasure of his body and hers. She leaned down to press her mouth to his and the tension exploded, sending her quaking and clenching around him. And she saw when he let himself go over and they shook together.

THEY STOPPED AT THE gate between his grandmother's and her grandfather's property. Paige leaned over to kiss him.

"Come over?" Zach asked.

"We just had sex an hour ago," she said.

"I'm not talking about sex. Well, okay, maybe I am." He grinned. "Just come in for a while. I like it when you're around."

"I can't," she said. "I need to get in and make sure Granddad's okay. It's why I'm here, remember?"

"I suppose." He pressed a soft kiss on her. It had none of the intense zing of their usual touches. It was just…sweet, she realized. Sweet and immensely comforting.

"Good night, Wild Thing."

"Good night."

There was a buzz going through her, keeping her feet from completely touching the ground as she rounded the path that led to the house.

And came down to earth with a thud.

Lyndon stood there, leaning on his cane, watching her through the gathering dusk. Lyndon, who'd clearly been there to see their parting. He shook his head and turned back to the house.

For a moment she froze, feeling as if she was sixteen

again and breaking the rules. Except that she'd never broken the rules when she'd been sixteen. She'd never run around with bad boys.

She was now beginning to think that was a pity.

When she got inside, Lyndon was sitting in his easy chair, staring into space. He said nothing at first, just studied her as she came in and sat.

"You got some sun today."

"We were outside," she said.

"You and that Reed woman's grandson."

"His name is Zach, Granddad."

He just shook his head. "I'm trying to think of the words to say, but everything I come up with is a cliché. Things like 'I thought you were smarter than this' and 'I can't believe I didn't see this one coming.' The thing is, just because they're clichés doesn't mean they aren't true." His smile held no humor. "I did think you were smarter than this. How long have you been fooling around with him?"

"Not long. Since last Friday." She paused. "Granddad, I—"

"He's why you decided to support this ridiculous museum effort, isn't he?"

"Yes and no."

"What does that mean?" he demanded.

"I'm not supporting it because Gloria's related to Zach. I'm supporting it because I believe in what she's doing. But if it hadn't been for Zach, I would never have found out about it."

"What a coincidence," he said sharply.

A spark of irritation went through her. "What's that supposed to mean?"

"Any idiot can see the advantages for him in this relationship. But for the life of me I can't figure out what's in it for you, taking up with that bum."

"He's not a bum." She said it and meant it, realizing she'd once thought the same thing.

"He is a bum. And you're better than that. Certainly better than taking up with a drifter who lives off his grandmother."

"He's not living off her. He's visiting."

"For a month?"

"I'm staying with you for a month," she reminded him.

"You've got a career."

"So does Zach."

"Doing what, hustling pool?"

"Playing guitar."

"That's hardly a career."

Anger flashed through her and she rose. "So he plays guitar. Gloria did burlesque. I'm an interior designer. Just because we don't hold one of those jobs you approve of doesn't make us worthless," she flung at him. "Gloria's trying to make a difference, and you don't want to let her because she doesn't measure up to your standards."

"You know, I saw Gloria Reed's pinup when I was in the war," he said quietly.

It took the wind right out of her sails. "You did?"

He nodded. "I joined up the day I turned eighteen. Didn't tell my family. My father and I were butting heads. He wanted to pull strings for me, get me a sweet spot. Well, I didn't want any special treatment. I signed my papers and they sent me to the PI." He shook his head. "When you're young, you think you know it all, but I still wouldn't change what I did."

"It must have been hard," she whispered.

He didn't answer. "A fellow in my squad had that pinup of Gloria Reed. It didn't look like she was posing, it just looked like a picture your girl back home might send you. I used to look at her every night and think that killing and living in the stink and the heat and the bugs was okay if it meant that we were doing what we could to keep girls like her safe."

He sighed. "And then the war ended. We got processed out through San Francisco. I was walking the waterfront when I saw it, big as life, outside a burlesque house—her picture on the marquee. 'Now appearing, Gloria Reed.'" He looked suddenly tired. "People disappoint you," he said. "Just don't expect too much from this Zach."

"Do you know why Gloria went into burlesque?" Paige asked gently.

"No, and I don't want to."

"I think you should. The pinup shot was an accident— a photographer driving by her family's farm. But another guy who came to town got her in trouble, a guy who told her she was special and he loved her and wanted to marry her. So then she had a baby to take care of. She hadn't even graduated high school. Burlesque was the only way she knew to make a living.

"And I know you don't think much of that, but she took care of her people. I think that's something to be proud of. Now she's trying to take care of people again. So she broke some rules. You ask me, that kind of rule-breaking is the right thing to do. And if just once you'd talk to her, really talk, without just being angry about what she did all those years ago, maybe you'd feel the same."

She rose and kissed his forehead. "I'm sorry I didn't tell you about Zach, Granddad, but I'm not sorry I'm doing it. It's funny the things you find when you look in unexpected places."

13

"A LITTLE TO THE LEFT," Paige instructed.

Zach shifted the poster he held against the eggplant-colored wall a fraction.

"No, I mean more."

"You said a little."

"I meant a bigger little."

He shifted it again.

"Inches, I mean."

"I did move it inches."

She held her hands apart in the air.

Zach stared at her from under his brows. "Why didn't you say you wanted it moved over a foot?"

"It's not a foot. It's only a couple of inches."

"Okay, is this like the color thing?" he asked with a glower.

"All right, don't get all riled. This is good," she said, making a quick mark on the wall. "After all, we can always move them later if we don't like it."

He gave her a double take. "Speaking on behalf of the painting staff who just spent two days climbing up and down ladders, that's a really bad idea."

"Look at it this way—you can use it as material for a new song. 'Well I got up this morning and I painted me some walls,'" she sang as she brought him another picture to hang.

"Maybe not."

"Really?" she asked, disappointed. "I thought I had something going there."

"Don't give up your day job."

Gloria walked in. "Oh, this looks wonderful, you two."

Paige put her hands on her hips and took a look around. "It's getting there. So you like it?"

"I think it's going to look beautiful. And I like the chaise," she said, running her hand over the fabric.

"It's supposed to mirror the poster." Paige pointed to a print leaning against the wall that heralded the arrival of the Columbia circuit show with extra-special guest, the talented Tessa LaFleur. LaFleur, a ravishing blonde with come-hither eyes, lay along a chaise, a white robe draped strategically over her.

"She was something, wasn't she?" Gloria asked. "She could play an audience like you've never seen, spend ten minutes just taking off a glove. Taught me a lot." She turned to the closet. "I've got that costume here somewhere."

"It's not one of the ones we've put in fixtures," Paige said, pointing to the stack of Plexiglas boxes.

"It might still be in the back." Gloria dived into the closet and rummaged around. "One of Sally Rand's fans," she said, poking her head out to hand it to Paige.

"I think I saw one of Tessa's costumes the other day," Paige said, waving the two-foot fan through the air and feeling the breeze against her face.

"Which day was that?" Zach asked, and she could feel her cheeks heat.

She threw him a dirty look. "Oh, earlier," she said vaguely as Gloria came out with the plastic-swathed robe.

"Ta-da." She unzipped the storage bag and put her hand inside. "White silk," she said reverently, showing it to Paige. "She used to wear it over a black velvet sheath that had all these tear-away parts. She'd strip them off, still wearing the robe so the dress got shorter and shorter underneath and then it was a bra and G-string and even less, until all she had on was that. And then—wham!—it came off. Va va voom," she added.

Paige looked up to see Zach's eyes on her. "Va va voom," she said, setting the fan down and leaning over Gloria to take a look. And then she sniffed. "What's that smell? Lavender?"

"And cedar. I like it better than mothballs."

"It's in beautiful shape," Paige said.

"Oh, it is. They all are. I used to try them on every couple of years just for the memories. Stopped doing that a couple of years ago, though." She gave a rueful smile. "Everything's moved to a new location, if you know what I mean."

Paige grinned. "Happens to us all. So I guess you always knew you'd do the museum if you took care of the costumes like this."

"I didn't really know. It just kind of seems to me that things shouldn't disappear. Burlesque was part of the theater, part of America. And a good part, too. A clever part. It was the tease, not the strip, and not a lot of that. At the beginning, it was mostly musical numbers and comics." She gave a fond smile. "Skinny Joe Biggs, Delbert Morton, guys who could be so funny without ever once using a single word you couldn't say in church. Not that most of 'em spent a lot of time in church." She winked.

"Anyway, listen to me go on. What I came down here to ask you two was whether you'd mind if I went out today. I've got my weekly spa appointment for the works and I could really use a massage. I know the open house is tomorrow. I hate to leave while you're both here working, but I'm—"

"Still recovering," Paige said. "Go ahead and go. We've got it all under control."

"I feel like I should at least be lending moral support."

"A fresh eye would be even better. Go off for your spa day, and when you come back, we'll probably be done. You can tell us if it works."

"Would you mind?" she asked gratefully. "I'm just still sore, and they do this wonderful hot-stone massage and facial. Hey, maybe you should go, too."

"Later. Go, enjoy yourself." Paige shooed her out the door and turned to Zach. "Now where were we?"

"Moving things a little," he suggested.

"Oh, right. Okay, let's get the poster of Tessa up."

Zach eyed the ornate gilded frame and hefted it. "This one we need to get in place much more quickly."

"A big, strong guy like you, you can pick up that itty-bitty lil' thing, can't you? We only have two more to hang."

"I can hold it fine. I'm just saying I need some direction here," he grunted.

Paige folded her arms and studied it. "Over a little," she said.

WHETHER IT HAD TAKEN longer than necessary was a matter of opinion, but finally the posters were all hung. "All we need to do is get the furniture in place and we can take a break for a while," Paige said. She walked back from the chaise and stood with crossed arms, studying it. "Hmm."

"Hmm?" Zach echoed. "You know, I'm starting to learn that 'hmm' is a bad noise that usually means more work for me."

She gave him Bambi eyes. "It hurts that you'd say that."

"The truth does sometimes."

"It's just that I'm torn."

"About?"

"Which way the chaise should face. I mean, if we turn

it the other way, then people can sit on it and look at Tessa. Then again, if we keep it this way, you get a nice visual echo when you walk into the room. Assuming they notice."

"Assuming." Zach stood next to her, studying the picture.

From the wall, Tessa looked down.

What would it be like to feel the soft spill of silk on her naked skin? Paige wondered, her pulse speeding a little. Exotic. Erotic. Arousing. Tessa would do it in a heartbeat. Tessa would reach out and take the chance. And Zach was right—the thought of the risk only added to the excitement.

Taking a breath, Paige turned to him. "Out into the hall."

He stared at her. "What?"

She turned him around and gave his shoulders a push. "I said, outside. I'll call when I'm ready."

When the door closed behind him, she just stood, heart thudding. She couldn't say she was doing it because she was caught up in the moment or not thinking. She was doing it because she wanted to.

Because it turned her on.

She walked to the closet and opened it, bringing out the robe. Unwrapping it, she laid it over the arm of the chaise. So much for the easy part—now she had to undress.

It took only a moment for her to push off her shoes and socks and lay them neatly inside. Taking off her jeans wasn't so bad; with her shirt on, she still felt mostly covered. It was when she pulled her T-shirt over her head that she felt vulnerable for the first time.

How had they done it, those women, stripping off their clothing in front of a theater full of strangers? What kind of boldness did it take to put yourself out there like that? She studied Tessa's face, seeing the hint of challenge in the gaze. The same look that she saw on Gloria's face, that of

As each bit of skin was exposed by the white strands, he felt as though he were seeing it for the first time.

And he felt the searing tear of desire.

Of course he wanted her, he always wanted her, but somehow connected only by her pleasure, it was more intense than it had ever been.

Paige had never been so aware of her body in her entire life. The feathers stroked over her body again. A small thing, a subtle thing, and yet it felt like an electrical shock running through her. Arousal beat in her veins and yet he hadn't even touched her except with his hot, dark gaze and the fan.

She took a long, deep breath.

When he reached out again, she rolled her body back a bit, exposing herself more completely to his eyes, to his touch, though he only stroked her with the feathers. With her eyes closed, touch became magnified. The more soft the brush, the more it raised goose bumps.

And then she couldn't stand it anymore. She opened her eyes. "Please," she said. "Please."

And he set aside the fan, stripped out of his clothing and leaned in to fuse his mouth with hers until pleasure flowed, liquid and thick, like melted caramel.

The whisper of breath. The sliding rush of hand over skin. The utter sybaritic pleasure of naked bodies pressed together. They'd come together in urgency, in excitement, in temptation. Now, they came together in sumptuous sensuality amid the somnolent calm of afternoon.

Slowly, Zach traced his fingertips over the long, smooth arc of her body, following the trail he'd traced with the fan. In touching, he revealed her, revealed himself. They didn't speak but somehow they didn't need to. Somehow the languorous kisses, the deep stares conveyed all that needed to be said.

And when she explored him in return and coaxed a shudder from him, then another, she hummed in satisfaction. Though as yet unconnected in body, they were connected in sensation, because she felt his pleasure as though it were her own.

He pressed her shoulders back into the cushions of the chaise. They'd laughed at the Supper Club all those nights ago when she'd confessed her love of missionary, but when Zach slid between her legs and lay atop her, she sighed in wonder. The weight of a man, the glorious weight as he rose to fill her completely. And for a breathless instant they stared at each other, connected utterly by touch, body, vision. Then he stirred and began to move against her, slow and purposeful. She stroked her hands down his back, tracing the groove of his spine, slipping her hands down further to cup the marble hard rises of his buttocks. Oh, yes, the weight of a man, this beautiful dark-eyed man, connecting them together until she could no longer tell where her pleasure left off and his began.

It was one of those moments, Zach thought, those endless perfect moments to hold onto forever, encasing it in amber in his mind. He watched Paige's eyes and it was like he could see into her, like they were fusing together somehow in a way that went beyond physical. He watched as she reacted to every infinitesimal movement of their bodies, watched the slow, drugging pleasure come over her. He fought his body's demand to move faster because he wanted to draw it out, to make it last, to live in the moment for far longer than the brief seconds of orgasm.

And when he went, he wanted to take her with him. He wanted to feel her body tighten around him and know that he'd brought her there. He wanted to see the exhilaration take over, watch her eyes go unfocused with sensual overload. And he wanted to be in her, deep and hard, connected, part of her, taking the two of them where they were going together.

He clenched his teeth, willing himself one more stroke and one more, because he wanted her there with him. And then, when he felt her body begin its helpless shuddering, when she clenched around him, tighter and hotter than he'd ever known, he let himself go, let the orgasm go, let them come to each other.

14

LIGHTS BLAZED FROM every window of Gloria Reed's home. Car after car drove up, discharging laughing passengers in party clothes. Inside, a band played Dixieland jazz and guests mingled with cocktails, eating salmon tartar and figs wrapped in bacon. Flashes threw bursts of light as photographers from the local media roamed around snapping pictures.

Have a party, Paige had said to Gloria of the open house. *Make it an event, invite everyone you can think of.* And Gloria, with her unerring sense of occasion, had pulled it off. The old house probably hadn't seen so much life and noise and high spirits in decades.

In the end, Lyndon had consented to attend with Paige, if only to see the inside of the house again. He wore a jacket and neatly pressed gray slacks. No wheelchair this time; he walked through the wing leaning on his cane.

And he couldn't quite disguise the pleasure of being there.

"My father hosted a party for the British Minister of Finance when I was a boy," he said. "The whole house was lit up like this, candles and flowers everywhere. I remember my nanny brought me down just to look at it. All the women wore diamonds."

They walked into the main entrance hall and there stood Gloria. "Paige," she cried and swept up to her. "I've been waiting for you. Everything's going wonderfully."

Gloria had chosen midnight-blue velvet for her gown. With her hair swept up and sapphires around her neck, she looked somehow regal. "Why, Lyndon," she said warmly, catching his hands in hers. "Thank you for coming."

A quicksilver series of expressions chased over his face: surprise, pleasure, puzzlement and suspicion. And finally contentiousness. "I thought I should see what you've had my granddaughter slaving away on."

Gloria raised one blond brow. "Upset because she hasn't been around every minute to wait on you hand and foot?"

"I don't have her waiting on me," Lyndon retorted.

"Well, that's good. Go on—" she waved her hand "—take a look around, see what we're going to do."

"*If* you get permission."

"When we get permission," she corrected.

A waiter stopped by to offer Lyndon champagne, but he shook his head. "None of that buttering up. I'm here to get information."

"And I suppose it would kill you to relax and enjoy yourself, you old goat."

"Don't think I don't know what's going on here," he warned her. "You think you can jolly the neighborhood and get them to change their minds. Well, you won't get past me."

She squinted at him, hands on her hips. "Were you by any chance a Puritan in a past life?"

"Just the kind of mumbo jumbo I'd expect from you."

They were enjoying themselves, Paige realized suddenly. She doubted they knew it, and even if they did, they wouldn't admit it under pain of death, but there was absolutely no doubt watching the two of them that they found a certain zest in the sparring.

Still, that didn't mean it was going to help the current effort to have it go on during the open house. She caught

Lyndon's arm in hers. "Why don't you come with me and take a look at the exhibits?"

He stopped reluctantly, looking at Gloria. "I suppose that's why I'm here."

"Then let's go see them."

Paige ushered him toward the rooms with a little buzz of nerves. As late as that morning, she and Zach and Gloria had been working to get everything arranged just so. They'd been looking at it for so long by then, though, there was no telling if their judgment was sound. As a designer, Paige always preferred to walk away for a day or so before deciding whether a look was right. Unfortunately they hadn't had the luxury, so she substituted crossing her fingers and hoping.

When she walked through the door, she exhaled in relief.

It worked, she thought. The rooms weren't perfect—she was a designer, after all, not a curator—but the exhibits gave a flavor of the time, put the subject in context. She'd used hasty research and Gloria's recollections to build storyboards telling the history of burlesque, illustrating it with the posters, props, photographs and costumes from Gloria's collection. In the background played recordings of classic burlesque routines that Paige had managed to unearth on eBay.

And at the end, simple statistics highlighted the grim straits of many of the retired entertainers who'd once nightly filled theaters with laughter and whistles. But it wasn't just the numbers—photographs brought the statistics to life, photographs of cohorts, captured by Gloria in recent years.

Around the room Paige heard murmurs. People laughed at the comedy, admired Tessa's robe, smiled at the posters. It felt for all the world like a gallery opening—the guests were treating it as a show rather than an open house for a project they could pass or block.

It was exactly the reaction she'd hoped for.

"Well?" She looked at Lyndon after they'd toured the rooms at length and were back out in the hallway.

He looked lost in thought. With a little shake of his head, he turned to her. "The exhibit looks good. You're very talented, you know." His eyes met hers. "I don't think I've told you that often enough, especially with that fool crack of mine the other day."

"I knew you didn't mean it."

"That's no excuse. I'm sorry about it. I was just…surprised."

"Let's not talk about that right now. What's important is the museum. Now that you know more about it, does it change your mind?" She gestured at the hallway wall, where they'd displayed logistical information covering everything from traffic to expected hours.

"I just don't know. I need some—"

"Lyndon." Gareth James walked up, toothy grin gleaming in the light. "I see you're back up and around. I guess they can't keep a man like you down for long."

"I'm a tough old bird," Lyndon said.

Gareth turned to her. "And, Paige, of course." He caught up her hand to kiss it. "You're looking well."

"Nice to see you again," she said politely. She'd worn high-waisted white silk trousers paired with a russet-colored blouse and needle high heels that put her looking just slightly down at him. To her amusement, he stretched up to his fullest possible height after he noticed.

"What do you think of all this?" he asked, waving at the exhibits.

"I think it's an interesting display for a good cause," she said. "What do you think?"

"I'd love to get my hands on some of those posters."

"I don't think Gloria's selling, but if you're lucky, she'll do limited-edition lithos. Assuming the museum gets approved."

Behind her she heard Charlie and some of the other planning commission members greet Lyndon.

"Yes, well, there's that."

"What are the chances, you think?"

He shrugged. "I think it has commercial merit as far as supporting the tourist industry in town. I know Lyndon and the rest of the residents have their concerns about the project, so we're looking into it carefully in terms of impact. And, of course, a lot depends on the neighborhood at the planning commission meeting.".

Said like a politician, she thought—long-winded, detailed and almost entirely uninformative. "We should probably move along," she began, glancing behind her for Lyndon. He was nowhere to be seen, though. Perhaps a trip to the bar or the men's room, she thought, settling in to wait, but the minutes passed and he didn't return.

Frowning, she wandered over to scan the reception area.

"Excuse me, didn't I see someone who looked exactly like you having sex under a tree earlier this week?" Zach's voice murmured in her ear.

And, as always, she felt the little rush of eager excitement. She turned to him. "Hi."

"Hi." He leaned in toward her.

"You can't kiss me hard," she warned him. "I've got on lipstick."

"I'll be careful."

The quick brush of lips shouldn't have made her heart thud faster. They'd done more, oh so much more. And yet somehow the simple touch resonated through her more than any of it.

"We pulled it off," she said, looking out over the crowd of people.

"I guess we did."

"You think it's going to turn the trick?"

"I don't know, but it was fun while it lasted, pardner."

It had been, she thought as he smiled down at her.

And suddenly she realized that something important had changed. She and Zach had been together, a team, the hours that had made up the week and a half somehow adding up to far more. And as they'd been working, focusing on the goal, she'd come to depend on him as part of her day, on his smile, his quiet kisses, his ability to make her laugh. Him.

Alarm flashed through her. She'd fallen for him, a man who didn't even have a clue what came next on any given day.

A man who liked it that way.

This wasn't supposed to happen. It had been safe to have the affair with Zach because there was no way it could go anywhere—he didn't belong in her world and she didn't belong in his. It wasn't supposed to be anything serious, just something to do while they were both in town. Instead it had become far more. How much, she didn't even want to think about, couldn't.

She forced herself to take a deep breath. Liking Zach, caring about him, wasn't the end of the earth. That was one thing she'd learned from living in his world—not everything had to be worked out in advance. Sometimes you could just let things be.

That was the challenge.

She shook her head briskly. "I have to go."

Zach blinked at her in surprise. "What's the hurry?"

"I need to find Lyndon. I got talking with someone and he disappeared."

"He's been taking care of himself for a lot of years. I think he'll probably be okay."

"I know, but he's my date."

"Ah." Zach reached out to tangle his fingers with hers. "Can I be next in line?"

"Umm…"

This time when he leaned in to kiss her, he lingered until desire began to chase through her. When he raised his head, she could only look at him blankly.

"Well. Uh, I'm going to go track him down."

The slow smile spread over his face. "And I'll be right here."

Lyndon wasn't in the upstairs galleries. He wasn't in the reception room. He wasn't in the hallway or on the back terrace or in the first exhibition room.

Then she walked into the second room and stopped.

He sat on a cushioned bench at the far end, alone. Both hands rested on his cane. On the wall before him was the enlarged version of Gloria's pinup.

They'd included it at the end of the sequence because it evoked images of sweetness and because it was a part of who Gloria was. To place it in context, Paige had surrounded it with images of its time: GIs walking onto steamers, families clustered around the radio, USO dances, Churchill and Roosevelt.

And Gloria, forever young and innocent, looking back from her white fence, one hand shading her eyes.

Lyndon sat like a statue as Paige walked up. Sitting next to him, she saw the sheen in his eyes. "I remember going to a USO dance while I was still Stateside, waiting to be shipped out," he said. "Pretty girls they had there, pretty girls." He fell silent. "It was about the last pretty thing I saw for a long while."

There were so many questions she wanted to ask and yet it was hard to know what to say. "Do you keep in touch with the other men you served with?"

"There aren't many left. John Ruffino, our sergeant, he's still around, down in Phoenix. The rest of the ones who survived are gone now. I was the youngster of the bunch." The ghost of a smile didn't dislodge the regret. "We lost most of my original squad in the fight for Peleliu. Gil— the one with the pinup—got hit by a sniper on Iwo Jima. It happened right in front of me."

Old grief echoed in his voice, stripped bare again. And there weren't any words that could ease it.

She reached out and laid her hand over his. "I'm sorry."

"It was what we had to do. No two ways about it and we got it done." He looked up at the image and the corners of his mouth curved. "Gil used to call this the picture of his future wife. Said he was going to go home and find himself a girl just like her. Boy, he'd have gotten a kick out of meeting Gloria."

"I bet he would have." She studied the lines on his face. "Listen, I don't want you to get too tired. Maybe we should call it a night."

He moved his shoulder. "In a bit, maybe. I'd just like to sit here a while longer."

She kissed his cheek. "Granddad, you take all the time you want."

THE OPEN HOUSE WAS long over, the glasses emptied, the caterers packed up and gone. Zach sat on the couch in the guesthouse, idly playing an old Clapton tune on his guitar.

Next to him, Paige rubbed her feet with a sigh. "The man who designed the high heel should have been sentenced to wear them until death."

"Hostile, aren't you?" Zach said.

"Try wearing them for five hours and see if you don't get hostile, too."

"You did buy them," he pointed out.

"Is it my fault? I'm a prisoner of fashion." She leaned her head back and put her feet up. "I'm so glad that's over. I am wiped. I don't know how Gloria kept going the way she did. Did you see her with that reporter from the paper? She had him eating out of her hand, especially when the guy from Sotheby's was practically begging her to bring him Tessa's poster for auction."

"Funny thing about people," Zach said. "Knowing something's worth a lot always makes them take it more seriously." He strummed a few chords.

"Speaking of things that are worth a lot, the guitar sounds nice."

"Thanks."

"Is the Sotheby's guy after it, too?"

Zach shrugged. "I'm sure they've probably auctioned them off over the years."

"Seriously?"

He smiled faintly. "Yeah, seriously."

"But it's just a guitar."

"And a Stradivarius is just a violin."

"Touché." She listened as he played a series of complicated harmonics, letting the sound ring out into the room.

"I thought the open house went well," Zach said.

"Now we cross our fingers and wait."

"Gloria's not so good at that."

"Neither am I," Paige agreed. "I guess we'll have to learn."

He reached out to toy with her hair. "Maybe I'll see what I can do to keep you busy."

"Hold that thought for an hour or so."

He raised his eyebrows. "That sounds like a challenge."

"Hold that thought for an hour or so," she repeated.

"Yes, ma'am." Grinning, he moved his hand and began strumming "I Walk the Line."

"Johnny Cash?" Paige slanted a look at him. "I wouldn't have picked you for a country music fan."

"Johnny's hip."

"I know. I read about him and Steve Rubin in that *Vanity Fair* article a few years back. You know, he got dropped by his label, too," she remembered. "Even after all his hits."

"You stay in the business long enough, I guess it happens."

"That probably doesn't help, though, does it?"

"Nope."

He started playing another song, one she vaguely recognized. "What's that?"

He smiled faintly. "'Nobody Loves You When You're Down and Out.'"

"You're not down and out. You're just getting ready for the next phase. Anyway, I'm sure Gloria would be happy to have you around for a while."

"Nope." He played a quick, flowing solo. "I've already stayed with her longer than I should have."

Paige waved a hand dismissively. "You've been helping her, so staying with her right now doesn't count."

"Exactly. But she's pretty well over the accident. After the commission's vote on Monday, it's time for me to get my act together and get out of her hair."

"I don't think she'd mind if you stayed longer."

"*I'd* mind. Besides, hanging around here just puts off the inevitable."

"What's that?"

He hit a short, sharp chord. "Figuring things out."

"Have you thought about session work? Just to pay the bills, I mean. Won't that open up some doors?"

He shot her a look. "Yeah, to more session work."

"At least you'd get paid for playing."

"I'm not holding my breath to play backing track on the latest SUV commercial."

"I'm not talking about that kind of work. Shoot, you hear all the time about Bono doing guest vocals or Keith Richards playing guitar on someone else's album. It's not something to look down on. It's a way to make a living."

"I couldn't do it here even if I wanted to."

"Of course not, but L.A. has a ton of studios." She sat up, warming to her topic. "There's Kev's friend. You've got an in right there."

"You don't even know what his friend does."

"I know Kev vouches for him. That's good enough for me. And there are about a bazillion clubs in town." Her eyes brightened. "There's nothing to stop you from forming another band, playing side gigs at night. The session stuff would just be your day job."

And that was what terrified him—stepping onto that slippery slope, the one where dreams skidded away. "I've never had a day job. All I've ever done is play music."

"And that's what you would be doing."

"*My* music," he emphasized. He knew what she was saying made sense, he knew that he was being petty and unreasonable, but he was powerless to stop himself.

"It would just be something to give you time to regroup. Do it for six months, a year, until you get a new recording contract."

But wasn't it the same as admitting he couldn't make it? And there was no guarantee that session work was a slam dunk. If he was going to be fighting for survival, he'd be better off doing it with his own music. "I'd rather go back on the road."

"But you're tired of that," she persisted. "And you can't make a living at it. This is the perfect answer. I'm not saying give it all up. I'm sure you'll get picked up by another record company. In the meantime, you get to stay in one place." She pressed her lips together for a moment and looked at him. "You could come down and live with me for a while, see how things work out." Her voice was casual; her posture was not.

See how things work out. Something told him she wasn't talking about the session work. "Live together?"

"Why not?" Her eyes watched him closely, gauging his reaction. "You? Me? It could be fun."

The thought flickered through his mind. Nights like this one, just sitting around and being together. Making love when it suited them. Waking with her, the way he'd never done. Having a home, the way he'd never had.

And letting her pay the bills for all of it. "Not an option," he said flatly.

And saw the flash of hurt in her eyes. "Well, gee, that was flattering."

"You know I didn't mean it that way."

"And you know I wasn't suggesting it as any kind of a commitment," she retorted, glancing away. "I'm fully aware that's not your speed."

"You don't know my speed," Zach replied, tamping down annoyance. "It just doesn't feel right."

"What do you mean it doesn't feel right? For God's sakes, Zach, I'm just offering you a place to bunk. Just like Gloria."

Except he wasn't having sex with Gloria, and Gloria wasn't pushing him to get a job. And Gloria didn't look at him with confusion and hurt on her face, confusion and hurt that he'd somehow put there. Suddenly he understood that in addition to figuring out what he was going to do with the rest of his life, he had to figure out what he felt for Paige, about the two of them together.

But not at the same time and not right now.

He rose and began to pace, dragging a hand through his hair. "Look, I know you mean well and in a lot of ways what you're saying makes sense. But right now all I feel is pushed. I can't do this on your time scale. I need to sort it all out."

"I'm not trying to tie you down," she snapped. "I was trying to help."

"And right now you could help by giving me some space to breathe," he returned.

"Fine. You want space, I can give you all kinds of space." She reached down to get her shoes and rose.

Goddammit, this was the last thing they needed. "Paige, wait…."

She turned at the door to give him a cool look. "I can't see any reason to." And she turned and walked out into the night.

15

"I KNOW, ALMA, BUT YOU asked to cancel the order. Now that you've changed your mind about wanting the chairs, we're going to be put at the back of the queue." Paige rubbed her forehead wearily. "Yes, I'll be in L.A. next week. We can meet then and take care of it. Yes, I'll call you as soon as I get home. Goodbye, Alma."

With the beginnings of a headache forming, Paige broke the connection. At least Alma paid handsomely for the privilege of driving her crazy. Zach Reed got to do it for free.

The headache pulsed and she got out a bottle of ibuprofen. Acting as though she was trying to trap him, plotting to tie him down. It wasn't as if she'd planned it all in advance, thought about how she'd spring it. It had just been an impulse, born out of a desire to help. She'd been trying to be nice. She cared about him.

It wasn't as though she was fool enough to really be in love with him.

And the last thing she needed was a roommate. She hadn't had one since college. She liked living alone, liked having her space. She liked peace and quiet. So there was something special about sitting on the couch and listening to him play. She didn't need it. Her iPod worked just fine.

Anyway, the reality was, they were two different people. Much as she enjoyed Zach, they'd probably drive each other nuts before long—she, the compulsive planner, he, Mr. Spontaneous. Sex on the beach was all well and good for a vacation fling, but where would she be, living with someone who thought that that was the way to live all the time?

That was the way to live all the time....

For a moment she was back at Cachuma Lake in the afternoon sunshine, with the sound of birds and the feel of his hands on her breasts, the hard, thick, insistent reality of his cock sliding in and out of her, every stroke bringing her closer and closer to the heat and flash and glory of—

"Stop it," she said aloud.

Stripping off her headset impatiently, she went into her bedroom and began to pack. It wouldn't hurt to get things folded away, to be ready to leave as soon as Lyndon was able to spare her. After all, the sooner she was gone, the less likely it was that she'd accidentally run into Zach, the easier it would be to fight off the memories.

Too many for merely three weeks. How had they all accumulated?

She thumped down her garment bag on the bed. So it had been fun while it lasted. It was time to come back to reality. She'd find a nice, stable man who wanted the same things she did, maybe even start thinking about settling down. It wasn't so out of the question. That was what normal couples did. Who was Zach Reed to act as though living with her was such a terrible fate? If she wanted, she could call any one of her exes—Marcus, for example—and have him back in a snap.

Only she didn't want Marcus.

There was a knock on the open door. Lyndon came in. "Never been so glad to see the back end of anything so much as that damned pink cast this morning," he said, rubbing his now-bare arm. Then he took a closer look at what she was doing. "Packing already?"

"Just getting things organized," she said of the stacks of blouses. "I thought I'd get a head start."

"I suppose it's time."

"Not right away. Maybe next weekend, if you think you'll be able to get around all right."

"You heard the doctor. I'm in good shape. Between Maria and the driver, we'll do fine. You need to get on with your life and your business. Although I'll miss having you around," he added.

"Dad will be here next month, so I'll definitely see you then. And I'll always be around, Grandpa. I haven't visited lately as much as I should. I'm going to be better about that."

"You have your own life."

"And you're a part of it. I'll be up more often. I have to come visit you. And Gloria."

"That woman," he snorted, but unconvincingly.

Paige clicked her tongue at him. "She's not so bad and you know it. Besides, you'd miss her if you didn't have her to snipe at."

"Hmph," he said. "Just make sure you give me back the key to the gate when you leave so I can lock it up. You might like going back and forth. I'm happy to stay on my side."

ZACH LAY UNDER HIS van, cursing as he tried to loosen a frozen bolt. The battered gray Ford had once been owned by a machine tool repair company and still bore its faded blue-and-white logo. Rust had started nibbling at the fenders. Scratches and dents pocked the sides. It wasn't pretty, but it had gotten him from place to place for more years than he cared to count.

And the miles had taken their toll. It needed a ring job and the bearings were going. As for the U-joints, they were shot, which was why he was currently flat on his back and

staring up at the undercarriage. Damned van, anyway.
Sometime soon he was going to have to spring for a new
one. Or newer, anyway, given the state of his finances.

One more thing to be pissed off about, one of many
things. He strained to break the bolt loose. The van had
needed new U-joints since he'd gotten to Santa Barbara
five or six weeks before. He'd meant to deal with it the
whole time.

Then again, he'd meant to deal with his life the whole
time and hadn't gotten to that either. Everything had been
taken over by the museum and the accident.

And by things with Paige.

The museum was out of his hands now; what would
happen, would happen. Gloria was almost completely recovered, so she wasn't his worry anymore, except in the
usual ways. And things with Paige…

Things with Paige were totally screwed up.

She was never supposed to get to be so important to him.
Always before, when things had gotten tough with women,
he'd figured the hell with it and walked. Well, he couldn't
say the hell with it this time. Paige had somehow become
part of the question of what to do with his life—and that
just made them harder to answer.

The fight they'd had still bothered him—maybe in part
because what she'd said was right. And yet the problem
was it wasn't that simple. You didn't just show up at an L.A.
recording studio and have them fall all over you offering
you work, not even with a track record. On the road his
name was on the marquee; in L.A. his name would be on
a sheet of paper—below the names of who knew how many
other guitarists.

Of course, on the road he would be without Paige. She
deserved a man who stuck around. Except sticking around

meant giving up his career and taking a flier on a day job. Granted, he might have a chance of getting something going with a new band.

As a sideline.

But what were the chances of it working out? What the hell were the chances that anything he might try to do with his music in the future would be any more successful than what he'd already done? He'd thrown everything he had into it. For years he'd made it the only thing he was about. Not that it had mattered that much, because there wasn't anything else he'd wanted.

But now there was Paige.

And yet moving to L.A. was saying that he'd given up, that it was over.

He cursed and slammed the wrench down.

"What the hell are you doing under there?"

Glancing between his feet, he saw a pair of open-toed red high heels that could only belong to Gloria. Perfect. "Writing my memoirs, what do you think I'm doing?" Shrugging his way out from under the van, he headed toward his toolbox. The very last person he needed to talk with was Gloria, who had a bloodhound's nose for anything that was bugging him.

"What's put you in such a great mood?"

"Oh, you know me, just high on life," he said. Metal clanked against metal as he rummaged around for his socket wrench.

She crossed her arms and studied the van. "You know, this beast is on its last legs. When are you going to break down and let me buy you a new one?"

"How about never?"

"Eventually I'm going to wear you down, we both know it. It would save us both a whole lot of grief and time if you'd just say yes now."

And the last of his patience evaporated. "Gloria, I know you mean well, but give me a break, will you? I'll buy a new one when I'm damned good and ready." Scowling, he headed back to the vehicle.

"Watch that mouth of yours, kiddo. When family offers to help you, you don't spit at them."

"Family should learn when enough is enough."

"*Family* should learn to appreciate the fact that he's got people who give a damn," she retorted. "Now what's the problem? Because I've got a pretty good idea it's not your van."

"The problem is my life, and I'd get it worked out if people would just leave me the hell alone." He sat down and slid his way back under the van.

"People?" One red shoe tapped. "What people?"

He clenched his teeth and strained against the bolt. "Nobody," he said explosively as it broke loose.

"Nobody, huh? That nobody wouldn't happen to live next door, would she?"

"You know what, Gloria, it's hard to hear you under here." He ratcheted out the bolt, squinting as a sprinkle of dirt from the van's undercarriage drifted down onto his face.

"That's all right, I can hear you just fine. By the way, the planning commission hearing is in about two hours. *Nobody's* going to be there, of course, but you might want to take a shower anyway."

He moved out from under the van and stared up at her. "You're a meddler, Gloria Reed."

"Dontcha love it?" she said, grinning.

THE WOODEN PEW-STYLE seating at the Santa Barbara Council Chambers was nearly full. Sunlight streamed in through wide windows hung with thick red velvet curtains.

At the front, the seven-person planning commission sat on a raised platform, looking sober and focused. A podium and microphone in the middle allowed audience members to speak and be heard.

Paige shifted on the wooden seat next to Lyndon, searching for a comfortable position. So far, there had been none of the vitriolic protests that she'd been led to expect, no placards, no shouting or hissing. Those who'd spoken up had mostly raised concerns they wanted to see resolved rather than demanded the end of the project.

And Lyndon had sat quietly at her side.

"Aren't you going to say anything?" she'd asked.

"I'm just going to listen for a while," he'd said. "See how it goes."

And now it was through and he still hadn't given a firebrand speech.

At the front, his friend Charlie cleared his throat. "We've heard from everyone who wished to speak. We're going to take a break and make our decision. We'll reconvene in fifteen minutes. If we recommend to approve, there will be a ten-day period of appeal. At the end of that time we'll have a binding decision. Thank you all for coming."

Bemused, Paige rose to see Gloria coming down the aisle toward her. "Paige." She gave her a hug. "This is going to be the longest fifteen minutes I've ever sat through."

"You can do it." Paige hugged her back, trying not to see the man beside her. She couldn't exactly ignore him, though. "Zach." She nodded to him as she stepped away from Gloria but didn't offer to shake hands.

Gloria flicked a glance at Lyndon. "You didn't say anything at the hearing."

"Was I supposed to?"

"Hell, I figured you'd at least get up and vent your spleen. Talk about the bougainvilleas, maybe."

"I didn't feel a need," he said.

Gloria gave him a suspicious stare. "Have you already sent in your twenty-page, single-spaced typed appeal?"

"The commission knows my opinions on the matter," Lyndon said neutrally.

"Well, I'm very optimistic about getting the variance," she announced.

"Excuse me." A young woman stood at her elbow. "I'm a reporter for the *Santa Barbara Chronicle.* I'd like to chat with you both a minute to get your comments."

Gloria and Lyndon glanced at each other. Gloria nodded. "Certainly."

"I'm going to go outside and get some air, Granddad," Paige said and turned up the aisle.

And Zach followed her. "Can I talk with you for a minute?" he asked as they reached the hallway.

She closed her eyes and opened them before turning. "Sure. Let's move out of the doorway."

On the wall, the dignified faces of the mayor and the deputy mayor looked out of framed pictures. Paige crossed her arms. "What's on your mind?" She refused to notice how good he appeared, how familiar.

How essential.

And tense and uncomfortable. "The other night." He cleared his throat. "I owe you an apology."

It was the last thing she wanted to hear. "There's nothing to apologize for. You're entitled to live your life as you choose. I should have kept out of it."

"You were trying to help."

"And you made it pretty clear you didn't want it."

He exhaled slowly, putting his hands on his hips and

looking down. "Paige… There's a lot of big stuff going on right now for me, a lot of changes. And I don't necessarily deal with them well. Getting the boot, losing my band, trying to figure out what I do now…" He hesitated. "Getting involved with you."

Words meant different things to different people, Paige reminded herself, even as she felt a jump of hope. "Getting involved?"

"It's turned out to be a lot more than I expected," he said simply. "It wasn't supposed to. I figured maybe I could shut it off. But all I've done for the last two days is miss you. And think." He looked at her. "I've been thinking a lot. What you said the other night about the day job? I was kind of a jerk about it, but you were talking about some stuff I just really didn't want to deal with."

"No kidding."

"That didn't mean you weren't right. Look, I know I'm on shaky ground musicwise." There was a defiant look in his eyes. "I don't know what, if anything, is ever going to happen. I could hit big tomorrow, but the chances are pretty high I won't. That's what I was talking to the other night, not you. I'm sorry it came out the way it did."

"It's not the end, Zach," she said softly. "It's just a chance to maybe do something a little different."

He gave a faint smile. "I tend to focus on the specifics. Speaking of which, you said something else when you were talking about the session work. Something about me going to L.A." He paused. "About us living together. I didn't react well to that either."

"I noticed."

"That would be a big change, too. I've never lived with a woman before. I haven't even lived in one place consistently for a long, long time."

Her cheeks felt hot, her hands icy-cold. "It was just an idea. A place for you to stay."

"You know it's not that simple," he said impatiently. "Living together means something here. I care about you. I want to be with you."

There was an almost painful pressure in her chest. "So you want to come to L.A. and live with me?"

He jammed his hands in his pockets. "I'm a loner, Paige. I've never tried to do an *us* before." His eyes were almost angry as he looked at her. "And I don't know that I'd be any good at it, but I want to try. Will you give it a chance?"

And suddenly the pressure was gone and a whole world of possibilities opened up in front of her. She took a breath, feeling relief turn into anticipation, joy, exuberance. "Okay. Let's do it."

She started to step toward him just as Gloria came out of the council chambers. "They're coming back in," she called to them.

And when the commission voted to approve the variance, it just seemed like a good excuse to start hugging people in celebration, beginning with Zach.

16

THE HIGHWAY LOOKED different, Paige thought as she headed down 101 to L.A. It looked different than when she'd returned to L.A. after the accident and different still than when she'd driven home with Zach. Those times, she'd been driving back to her home.

This time she was driving to her future.

Lyndon, predictably, had been appalled to hear of their plans. "You're letting him move in with you? He doesn't even have a job."

"He will," she'd promised. Zach would, she was certain. He had contacts; he'd already talked with his booking agent. Things would work out for him.

Things would work out for them.

She rolled down the window and turned the radio up. The idea of living together gave her a feeling of anticipation that was partly nerves, partly excitement. She supposed Lyndon was right—it was crazy to move in with a man she'd known for a month. Then again, what the heck? Why not take the leap and learn sooner rather than later if they could make it work?

She'd never expected to live with a man before marriage—not that she'd thought there was anything inherently wrong with it, it just wasn't for her. Now it seemed like the right thing to do.

She pressed on the accelerator. It was time to get there and get started.

LYNDON FAVREAU WALKED slowly through the grounds of his estate. Daily he stolidly worked his way through the rehab exercises assigned to him by a physical therapist who could have taught a Marine drill sergeant a thing or two. This was work.

These afternoon walks, though, they were pleasure, a reminder that even though his body was aging, he could still be hale. He would never have admitted just how difficult moving around was for him. Better to concentrate on the sounds of the birds.

Ahead of him he heard a stream of cursing and looked out to see Gloria Reed in a gardening hat and jacket, staring down over the white privacy fence.

He took his time ambling up to her. She looked hot and disheveled and mad as a wet hen. "Something wrong?" he asked.

"Of course something's wrong. Would I be in here if it wasn't?" she demanded. She'd wedged herself into the bougainvillea so that she was leaning over the fence, stretching down toward the ground as far as she could, with clippers in her hand. "I dropped my damned glove. Would it be too much trouble for you to hand it to me? Or do I need to go get a hanger?"

"Get a hanger?"

"To pick it up."

He looked around and spied the white-and-green glove on the ground. Ignoring the throb of protest from his ribs, he bent carefully down and reached for it, dusting it off as he rose. "What are you doing out here?" he asked, handing it to her.

"Oh, I saw the bougainvillea was creeping up. I didn't

want you to blow a gasket over it. My gardener's on vacation for a couple of weeks and it's a nice day, so…" She shrugged.

"So you came out here to trim it for me?"

She scowled. "Don't get all excited. I'm just trying to be neighborly after you let the museum go through."

"I appreciate it."

"Right back atcha." They stared at each other, uneasy with the truce. With a shake of her head, Gloria went back to cutting bougainvillea.

Lyndon watched her. "I understand that grandson of yours is moving in with my granddaughter."

She snipped a runner off. "They were both over eighteen last time I checked."

"It's a mistake."

"I always figure life is a lot more interesting that way," she said unconcernedly. "It certainly was for me. Of course, you've probably never made a mistake in your life, have you?"

He touched the blunt ends of some of the bougainvillea branches that still poked up through the new foliage. "More than a few," he said. "More than a few." He cleared his throat. "So do you often go fishing over the fence with hangers?"

"Depends how heavy they are. Sometimes I have to go get the grabby tool from the gardener's shed."

"The grabby tool?"

"You know, one of those snake things with the hooky parts at the end?" She mimed clutching fingers.

"Ah. A grabby tool."

"I've got to do something. I figure if I ever tried to jump over, that gardener of yours would come after me with his pellet gun."

"Felipe doesn't have a pellet gun."

"So you say."

"Well, that puts you in a spot some, doesn't it?"

"I suppose so. A person would think the gate might be a good answer. Of course, I can't open it right now. If you were to, say, unlock it, then I could get my own gloves and not bother you. But I suppose you figure that would be a mistake, too."

Lyndon considered. "Possibly one of the interesting variety, I think."

She blinked at him. "What's that supposed to mean?"

He shook his head. "Absolutely nothing. Have a lovely afternoon, Gloria Reed." And he sauntered away whistling, leaving her staring behind him.

IT WAS ONE THING TO think about something, it was another thing to do it. Zach walked down the central hall of Paige's flat, the one that led from kitchen to living room to office to bedroom. The hardwood floor beneath his feet gleamed. He'd been there before but somehow it all looked different now. Or maybe he was seeing it with new eyes.

He was going to be living in her house. He wasn't at all sure how he felt about it. Added up, the decision made sense.

But it still seemed wrong.

"I'm almost sure I can offer you water," Paige called from the kitchen, "but anything beyond that, you're taking your life in your hands. We can go stock up later on."

"I'm cool for now," he said and continued to explore. The art on the walls was the real thing, he was guessing. Expensive. But then, for a woman like Paige, expensive was a whole other league than for him.

Something to get used to.

Behind the wheel of his van, the miles rolling away, he'd

felt as if he'd slid back into his old life, as if he was back on the road. A couple more hours driving and he'd pull up to a club and unload the equipment, do the sound check.

Instead they'd driven up to Paige's house.

So he was pacing around, looking at the apartment and trying not to get freaked out at all the subtle reminders of money. It shouldn't have been a surprise. He'd known all along that she lived a different lifestyle.

The problem was, he generally didn't think much about that kind of thing. Sure, Gloria was wealthy, but she hadn't been born to it, so there was always a sort of merry feck-lessness in her ownership of expensive goodies and homes, as though the two of them were just gypsies in the palace, waiting for the owners to return. Paige acted as if she just didn't notice her surroundings any more than she'd regis-tered her nifty sports car.

Something else to get used to.

Paige hurried out of the living room holding something yellow in her hands. Some of those sticky notes, he realized. "Now I've marked where everything goes. The movers should be here any minute, and I've got some calls I really need to return right now. Can you please make sure they get things in the right place?"

He looked at her in amusement. "You're kind of scary when you're organized, anyone ever tell you that?"

She grinned. "You ain't seen nothin' yet."

At the sound of the buzzer, they both looked around.

"That must be them." Paige rose and went to the intercom to buzz them in. "You got it from here?"

"Sure."

It started out as a thank-you kiss, but it swiftly went deeper. However uncertain everything else was, this was solid and true, the way she shivered when he touched her just so, the way the taste of her filled him with that red haze of wanting. And so he held on to it, took it deeper, feeling the connection between them strengthen.

The sharp rap on the door made them both jump.

"Oh," Paige said, smoothing her hair and straightening her shirt as she went to open the door.

"Paige Favreau?"

"That's me," Paige said.

The burly moving man looked at her just a fraction of a second longer than necessary. "I'm Danny. This is Antonio." Antonio wasn't as bulked up as Danny, but he made up for it in height.

"Great," Paige said. "I've got to do a couple of things, but this is Zach. He'll show you where everything needs to go. Any questions, ask."

The movers glanced from Zach to Paige as she walked away, trim and tidy in tan pants. "Let's get to it," Danny said and headed for the elevator with Antonio.

One piece at a time, they started carrying in the furniture Paige had loaned to Gloria. They didn't look at him and ask why he couldn't move his own damned furniture, though they probably wanted to. Their glances held a certain amount of envy. When one of them stumbled as they walked by carrying a chaise, Zach moved to help, but they shook him off. "We've got it. No need to bother. Sir," Danny added.

And they didn't have any questions for him, save the one unspoken one that hovered in the room: How had he stumbled into a sweet gig like this?

Zach wasn't set up to watch other people work. It made him feel at loose ends and he didn't like it, he didn't like it one damned bit.

And hell if he was going to let Paige give him money to

tip them. "Zach, it's coming from my business." She started back into her office. "Gloria's paying for it, trust me."

"Then you can pay me back," he said, pulling out his wallet. Of course, handing off a couple of twenties left him with less than a hundred bucks.

And not a gig in sight.

Suddenly the apartment seemed stifling. "I'm going down to my van and unload a couple of things," he said abruptly after they'd left.

"We just got here. Why don't you wait until it cools off?"

"I don't want the Les Paul sitting in the heat."

He didn't want to think what it cost to live there as he headed down the street toward his van. He didn't want to think how long it might be before he was making enough to shoulder his share of the load. Assuming he ever would. It was a well-to-do city neighborhood like any other— prosperous, settled.

And foreign as hell.

He was surprised that someone hadn't already called in his van as a suspicious vehicle. Surely anyone with a machine this old had to be up to no good. He got into the front seat to grab his cell phone off the console and saw the message light flashing. Two calls, he saw.

The first was from Kev, with the number of his friend with the studio. "He needs a guitarist. Says you can come in and audition next week. Lemme know how it goes, man." With a click, the message ended.

Audition, Zach thought. He hadn't auditioned since he'd been seventeen. He had a funny feeling that was going to change real quick, though. No telling how many he'd have to get through before he'd get work. If he was lucky, some of the contacts he'd been calling up in the last few days would come through. If not…

Suddenly the words of the next message had him snapping to attention.

"Zach, Barry. Need to talk with you about some things. Promising stuff, my man, very promising stuff. Give me a call."

He hit redial immediately.

"Creative Music Associates."

"Bonnie, Zach Reed."

"Calling for Barry?"

"Do I ever call for anyone else?"

"I keep thinking you might call for me one of these days."

"You know I'm married to my music," he said.

"All you musicians are," she tsked. "Hold on."

There was a click and Barry came on the line. "Hey, Zach, how's it going?"

"You tell me."

"Look who's in a hurry."

"That would be me, Barry," Zach replied shortly. "What's going on?"

"What's going on is I've been working the phones. Talked with some folks about you and it's good news."

"Commercial work or real music?" There were levels to which he wouldn't sink, but then again, Zach thought, looking down the street, he might not have a choice.

"Commercial or music?" Barry repeated in a baffled tone.

"The session work. What am I looking at?"

"Oh, hell, I don't handle session work. Talk to your booking agent. I'm talking about you, my man, your music."

And adrenaline vaulted through him. His music. No sessions playing someone else's backing. A new record company maybe, a new chance to finally, finally make the breakthrough. "Who is it?"

"It's still in play right now," Barry said, which Zach recognized sinkingly as Barry speak for nothing solid. "There are a couple of people I'd like to get you in front of, though."

"Did you send them CDs?"

"We need to do this live. Maybe your booking agent can set up some gigs while you're out there?"

That was more like it. "I'm down in L.A. right now. Where are they?"

"Nashville, for starters."

Zach frowned. "Country territory, Barry."

"There are some blues joints, as well. The thing is, there's a good chance I can get the A and R guys there."

"How good?"

"They've promised to try. We just need to get 'em scared, get 'em thinking if they don't sign you, they'll miss out."

"They're supposed to sign me because they want my music."

"Zach, man, they just need to hear you to love you."

"A showcase," Zach said, unwillingly feeling the hope flicker. "You want me to do a showcase that they'll maybe show up for." And maybe not.

"Hell, this business runs on showcases."

"I've got a track record, Barry."

"And if you do this right, you'll have a contract."

Scrape a band together, rehearse, blast across the country, all for the hope of playing for a couple of A and R men—if they showed. At seventeen, it had sounded breathlessly exciting. Now, almost twenty years later, all he could think wearily was that he shouldn't have to go through this crap anymore.

"Realistically, what are my chances?" he asked.

"All in your hands, my man. You know how to work an audience. They're yours and they don't even know it." As if sensing Zach's wariness, Barry's tone became more intense. "Come on, Zach, don't pass this one up. This is your chance to finally hit. You're the best-kept secret in the blues. It's time to get that secret out."

And fanned by Barry's flame, the embers of hope began to glow again.

Zach took a deep breath. "All right," he said. "I'm in."

STANDING IN HER LIVING room, Paige slipped out of the clothes she'd worn all the way from Santa Barbara, then shook back her hair with a rush of relief. Granted, she'd made good use of the local dry cleaner's, but after four weeks, she was sick to death of the outfit. She was sick to death of all the clothes she'd taken with her. Anyway, if she wanted to ambush Zach when he came back in with his guitar, she had in mind something more provocative than yet another set of silk separates.

They could finish his unloading later; right now there were more important things to do.

But when he came through the door, he wasn't carrying his guitars. He wasn't carrying anything.

Then again, she wasn't wearing anything.

"Lose your van?" She stepped in to slide her arms around his neck.

"Lose your clothes?" he asked in a cracked voice.

"I thought I'd save us some time," she purred, tugging at his shirt. "Occurs to me that moving can wait. We've got a bed to break in."

And she started to press a kiss on him, but he pulled her arms from around his neck. "Give me a sec," he said.

It wasn't precisely the effect she'd had in mind. "All tired out from the drive?" she joked, stepping back. She wasn't going to be embarrassed. This was the downside of spontaneity—you had to let the other person catch up.

But look at how many times he'd refused to listen to her protests. Look at how many times he'd seduced her. Now it was her chance to return the favor. "Maybe you should lie down," she suggested, running her fingers through his hair and leaning in to lick his earlobe. "Maybe we both should."

"No, but I just…let's not do this right now, okay?" he blurted.

She couldn't quite read his expression. Tension maybe, and underneath it glimmers of excitement. "What's going on, Zach?" she asked, starting to feel uncomfortable. Hugely uncomfortable. She turned for her bedroom.

"Wait, Paige." Zach caught her before she'd gone more than a few steps. "Hey, it's not that I don't want you. Hell, that's not possible, especially when you look like this. I just need to talk with you about something."

So much for spontaneous. So much for living on the edge. Instead of making love with abandon in her living room, she found herself wrapping her robe tightly around herself and belting it.

She sat on the couch. "So talk."

He waited a moment as though choosing his words carefully. "I just got off the phone with my manager."

And a cold, hard ball of tension formed in the pit of her stomach. "Your manager? The one you can never reach? What did he have to say?"

"Good news. He's been getting some nibbles from the record companies."

"What does that mean?" she asked, working to keep her voice steady. "Do you have to go meet with them?"

"Sort of. He's set up a little tour for me in the South, to get me in front of some A and R guys."

"A and R?"

"Artists and repertoire. The ones who sign bands."

"And you agreed to go."

"I agreed to go." His voice was tense, his eyes watchful, but she saw the excitement simmering in them. "My booking agent's trying to set up some gigs while I'm out so I'll make some money."

"You're going back on the road?"

He nodded.

It was like being sucker punched. Just when she thought they were going to get their chance, Zach's other big chance showed up. She didn't know how to feel. Happy for him? Despairing for them? A fool for ever believing that anything, including her, could ever matter to him the way his music did?

She rose and walked across to the windows to look down at the street below. "Congratulations. I guess this is really good news. So they're talking about signing you?"

She heard him stand. "Not yet. I might have a chance to impress the right guys, though, the ones who can make deals." The floor creaked under his feet.

"Might," she repeated. "So you're auditioning."

"It's called a showcase, but, yeah." With his hands on her shoulders, he turned her to face him, raising her chin with a fingertip. "It's a chance, Paige, maybe another contract." And everything in his expression begged her to understand.

"Where is it?"

"Nashville, believe it or not. I've got to scare up a band there who can tour with me."

She wanted to understand, she wanted to be happy for him, but underneath it all she just felt dizzy with shock. "But what about the sessions work that Kev was helping set up for you here? He pulled in a favor. Can't you pull together a band here in L.A. and get in front of a record company?"

"I can't risk it," he said. "I might not get another chance like this. I've been at the end of the road, here, don't you understand?"

The end of the road. Funny, she'd thought it was a beginning.

Zach put his hands on her arms. "I know this looks really bad. I just can't…I can't walk away without trying. It's a long shot, I admit it, but it might be my last one. And if I don't take it, it's always going to dog me."

He was leaving for a sliver of a hope of shaking something loose. And once he was back out on the road, what were the chances he'd come back? It was like seeing him pass by on a boat that never landed, watching him drift closer and closer, then just when she thought he'd come to her, seeing him draw away, sliding gradually out into the distance.

Knowing he was going to be gone.

She was losing him, she thought, before she'd ever really had him. She moistened her lips and walked away, turning back to him. "How long?"

"I don't know. Barry thinks he might be able to get them to show in a couple of weeks."

"Might?"

"It's never a given with A and R guys until it happens, and sometimes not even then. Anyway, two weeks doesn't give me a hell of a lot of time. My booking agent says she can scare up three or four last-minute gigs for me. Maybe more. Anyway, I need to head out for Nashville if I'm going to have time to rehearse. I'm really sorry to just turn around and leave like this."

Paige swallowed through a painfully dry throat. "That's all right. You never really got here, anyway."

"What do you mean?"

"This was never your thing. It's the dream that drives

you. That's what matters to you, Zach." The only thing, the same as any musician. And there was no way she could ever compete.

"I don't have any dreams," he said impatiently. "I don't care about being a rock star. Don't you get it? All I want to do is play my music. I just want to give it one last try. If it doesn't work, I'm done."

And now anger billowed up. "Oh, come on, Zach, stop fooling yourself. You are never going to think that it's done. You're always going to want to be out there, thinking the next time might be the one." It was simple, it was crystal clear.

It was excruciating.

"It's my life." His voice was soft. "It's what I love."

It's what I love. And suddenly she understood why she felt the pressure in her chest, suddenly she understood what she'd already known. It was like looking at a Hidden Pictures page and seeing the objects finally come clear.

She was in love with him.

And she wanted more.

"I'm glad you love something," she said in a rusty voice. "Everybody should." And she couldn't let herself say the words, knew it was the wrong time, but they thudded through her, shattering her heart with every beat.

"I don't see why we can't make this work," Zach persisted. "So I go on the road for a while. I'll be back."

"For what, a weekend? A week? You've told me what that life is like. Come on, be realistic."

He caught her hands, looked at her, eyes intense. "Look, this thing with us, it's important to me. You're important to me. I don't want anyone else, and if I go on the road, I'm still coming back to you. We can make this work."

"How?" she demanded, turning away. "Making this

work means being together. It means the day-to-day stuff, sitting down to dinner, waking up together. It's not a half-hour call every night from whatever hotel you're in, wherever the hell you are."

"You could come with me some of the time."

"Did you forget that I've got a business here? I can't just walk away. I've got to be here. Day-to-day stuff, Zach. And you're not ready to say this is your life, anyway, not really." She stalked back and forth, staring at him. "Look at you, you're leaving before you ever even got here."

"It's a timing thing."

"And it's always going to be." Abruptly the anger evaporated. She walked up and put a hand to his cheek. "Look, I…" She stopped. "I care about you. I really want this, you and me, but it's the wrong thing at the wrong time. I don't want to be here keeping the home fires burning so you can come home once a month from living with another woman, even if that woman is music."

His brows drew down. "So, what, it's an ultimatum? My music or you?"

"I never flattered myself that there was ever a choice, Zach," she said aridly. "There's a point where you have to deal with the life you have, not the one that you want. Or I do, anyway. Let's just say that we tried it out and it didn't work."

"I don't want to lose you."

She kissed his forehead even as her heart shattered to dust. "You've got to lose something here, Zach."

I have.

17

SHE WEPT AFTER HE left, wept until she was exhausted. And then she drifted down into restless sleep, only to wake in the darkest hours of the night, cheeks wet with tears.

She gave herself the weekend. When the week started, the business of life would begin. But until that time, she'd draw up the drawbridge and unplug the phone. This was nobody's time but hers. Time to lick her wounds. Time to try to make sense of what had happened. Time to get through it and go on.

It had been so obvious, in retrospect, that the relationship couldn't have worked. It wasn't just that they were two such different people. It was that what he ultimately wanted was something she could never give him. And, she supposed, the reverse was true, because the man she truly wanted to spend her life with needed to see her, the two of them together, as more important than anything else in his life.

And yet, irony of all ironies, she loved him.

He could make her shiver and quake. He could make her laugh, have fun. He could teach her a new way of living, make her world a bigger place. But he could never make her central to his life and he could never be her center.

He could never love her back the way she needed him to.

And she wasn't willing to accept any less.

"OKAY, LET'S GO THROUGH it again. Blues in B flat. When you get to the bridge, watch me," Zach directed.

The drummer clicked off time and they launched into the song. After being with the same band for nine years, playing with a new group of musicians felt foreign, stiff. Granted, he'd played with the pickup group in Santa Barbara, but that had been casual, for fun as much as anything. This mattered. It had to be right because everything hinged on it.

He'd gotten a list of recommended session players when he'd hit Nashville; unfortunately funds and timing had dictated who he could actually choose. They were better than the Santa Barbara group, he'd give them that. Whether they were the band he'd choose to do a showcase with when his career was on the line, though, was a whole other question.

It was worth battling through the rehearsals, he reminded himself. It was worth running his charge card up to the limit to pay them. It was worth it for the chance.

He'd given up a lot to get it.

And just like that, Paige was back on his mind. However, that wasn't exactly unusual. At odd times he'd wonder what she was doing. Or he'd read something or hear something and make a mental note to tell her.

Or he'd lie awake at night, trying not to imagine what it would feel like to drift off with her in his arms. They'd never slept together. They'd sneaked sex here and there like high schoolers, but they'd never had a full night. They'd never woken up together in the morning.

And they weren't together now. He hit the strings with unnecessary force. It was a choice he'd never wanted to make, but he'd done what he had to. Music was part of him. He'd had to do it. He had to take the chance, and if she couldn't understand that, then she didn't understand him.

But he had a feeling she understood him a whole lot better than he wanted her to.

Then they were at the bridge and he moved off onto the solo until once again, at the same place as before, the rhythm guitarist muffed the transition.

In frustration, Zach chopped his hand, signaling a cut. "Okay, let's take a break. Back here in five."

He couldn't focus on Paige anymore. He had one chance and he had to make it work, no matter what it took.

After all, the price for it had already been way too high.

HAMMERING. SHE distinctly heard hammering. Gloria Reed sat by the pool, trying to ignore the emptiness she'd felt around the place since Zach had left, and raised her head to listen. Curious, she rose and traced the sound to the privacy wall.

And found Lyndon Favreau setting up planters on top of it. They needed little stilts added to keep them stable on the curve; that was the hammering she'd heard.

"Lyndon, what are you doing?" she asked with a frown.

He nodded his head. "Planter boxes," he said unnecessarily.

"I see them. It looks an awful lot to me like you're putting those planter boxes up on top of this wall, but for the life of me I can't think why."

"I thought they'd look nice."

"Do you have a fever?" she demanded.

He touched his forehead. "Not that I know of. I might be having heart trouble, though, if you don't stop walking around like that."

"Oh." She glanced down at her blue maillot, and for the first time in a good sixty years she blushed. "I was sitting by the pool."

"I sure hope so."

"I heard a noise."

He nodded. "Sorry to disturb you. I thought maybe this would take care of things until it grows back."

The boxes, she saw, had bougainvillea cuttings in them. "You old coot, did you buy planter boxes for this entire fence?"

"Not quite all. The part up front here, anyway. When your vines grow back, I'll take them away."

She stared at him. "Well, I'll be damned if you aren't a one," she muttered.

"A one what?"

"I don't know," she said aggrievedly. "You hate the bougainvillea."

"I might be changing my mind. I've been doing that some lately."

"Well." She put her hands on her hips and stared at him. Lyndon went serenely about his business. "Well," she repeated.

"You already said that," he pointed out and put a box in place right before her with a clunk.

"I'm working on more."

"Take your time."

"It's a nice thought," she offered. "How about that?"

"It's a good start."

"If you weren't such a contrary cuss, I'd invite you over for an iced tea, even if you did kill my Bentley. Your gate is still locked, though. Too bad."

Lyndon leaned on the wall and looked at her for a long time. Then he reached in his pocket and brought out a key. "I believe I have a way to fix that," he said, clicking loose the padlock and tossing it onto the ground.

"Well, if you aren't a one," Gloria murmured again.

"A one what?"

"Give me time," she said, swinging open the gate. "I'll think of something."

THE TURNOUT WAS THIN, even for a Thursday night. A group of city-league softball players clustered around the pool tables in back, mostly focusing on drinking beer. Others stared at the televisions, where the basketball players lunged at the basket.

"Zach Reed, my man!"

Zach looked over to see Barry Seaton heading toward him. The beard on Barry's cheeks did little to disguise his jowls. He'd been a big fan of the Johnny Cash biopic when it had come out and had taken on the man-in-black style with enthusiasm, apparently a believer in the slimming abilities of the color. Zach wondered if anyone had ever told him it didn't work when you were five foot six and built like a fireplug.

Barry seized his hand and pumped it. "Zach, I want you to meet Joshua Wrentham of Peach Records down in Atlanta. Josh, meet Zach, our blues guy."

Wrentham looked all of twenty-five, maybe, with a soft, disinterested handshake. "Joshua," he corrected. "Nice to meet you." Zach had the feeling that even as the guy was saying the words, he was looking over the room for another prospect.

It was a chance, Zach reminded himself, pushing down the irritation. It was a food-chain thing, and currently he was down with the amoebas. No point in reacting—you didn't get anywhere by ticking off the A and R guy.

Meanwhile, Barry was on a roll. "We've got Zach here with the blues, and if you're looking for something a little more Southern-fried, we've also got Loudon James and the Alabama Playboys. Joshua, meet Loudon."

Rawboned and barely old enough to vote, Loudon James was dressed in the Western-cut-suit-and-cowboy-hat combo that was the Nashville uniform.

"Okay," Barry said, sitting Wrentham down. "Let's get Zach up to play a few songs for you and then we'll finish with Loudon."

Zach snapped his head around to stare at Barry. "You didn't tell me I was going to be the opening act," he said under his breath.

"Someone's got to go first. You lost the coin toss," Barry said equably.

Lost the coin toss his ass, Zach thought as he stepped onstage and plugged the amp cord into his Les Paul. Barry had dragged him all the way out to Nashville as an opening act for his new best boy. Well, it was time to show them that veterans knew a thing or two.

"Okay," Zach said to the band. "Let's do it."

It was hard and fast, driving blues that grabbed the crowd by the throat and yanked them on the dance floor. His bad luck that there was no crowd, let alone one that danced. All he had to work with were the city leaguers. All he had to do was make it not matter.

That was a job, though, when he was playing with a new band. He and Angel and Rory had been friends. They'd been together long enough that the energy just flowed through them all when they started playing, and the music flowed, too. That feeling, that flow, was part of what made the music worth doing.

Still, the first song sounded pretty tight, he thought.

And then he checked the front table with Barry and the A and R guy to see their reactions and his jaw tightened. They weren't looking his way. They didn't even appear to

be listening. Wrentham was flirting with the waitress, and
Barry was busy picking lint off his lapel.

Zach suppressed a surge of annoyance. It was okay, he'd
wake them up. If they wanted it to be a "show me" challenge,
then show them he would. He led the band into the second
song, a slow and nasty blues number that showed off his
vocals. At the bridge, he ripped off into a fluid, wailing solo
that glided on along over the rhythm line in counterpoint,
feeling the good throb of the bass, feeling it work.

When he looked over again, the two of them were deep
in conversation with Loudon. Barry was waving his hands
around—doing his sell, Zach realized. The sell that was
supposed to be for him.

If he got any more pissed, he was going to lose it, so
instead he did what he always did when things got rough—
he closed his eyes and dived into the music and tried to
make it not matter. He thought about the nights it had been
good. He thought about the shows where everything
clicked—the audience, the band, the sound—the shows
where he hadn't worried about impressing some kid. All
he'd worried about was the music.

And he thought about the night Paige had shown up.
She'd sat there out in the audience, staring at him, moving
to the notes he played until it had been as though they
were touching, as though they were making love. And
then they had.

Getting involved with her was supposed to have been
just another affair, like so many he'd had over the years—
diverting but never more important than his career. Instead
Paige had come to matter to him more than any woman
ever had. More than almost anything in his life.

Focus, dammit. Here he was in the middle of a last-
chance showcase, thinking about Paige once again. He

couldn't afford that. He had to stay in the moment, not get sidetracked. He had to focus on what mattered, he had to dial in on the most important thing.

And suddenly it hit him with the force of a blow—the most important thing was Paige.

So why the hell was he standing here?

Abruptly he opened his eyes. Across the room, two of the city-league players compared skinned knees and other injuries. Barry was still nose to nose with Loudon. The A and R guy was gone.

And frustrated, distracted, Zach screwed up the chord change. The rhythm guitar player snapped his head around to stare at him. No one else noticed, though. It didn't matter a whole hell of a lot.

And wasn't that a sad statement on his life?

For the first time in his career, he was happy to finish a set. He walked off the stage and over to the table. Wrentham was back, talking with Loudon and Barry.

"...maybe get you in the studio next month—"

They broke off and looked up when Zach approached. He itched to just walk out—just walk out, get on the road and drive to Paige, as quickly as he could. But he was here for a reason. If he were smart, he'd schmooze, see if he could turn the opportunity into something. Those were the rules: the A and R guys had to suck up to the big acts, so the smaller acts had to suck up to them. And so it went. He knew the rules, he knew the game.

But he just couldn't make himself care.

Taking a deep breath, he tried to salvage things. "You guys hear everything you wanted?"

"Why don't you sit down and take a load off, my man?" Barry asked genially. "Let Josh here tell you what he thinks while Loudon's getting ready to play."

Wrentham gave him that bored look, and suddenly Zach knew that he didn't give a damn what Josh Wrentham had to say because there was no way in hell he was going to let Wrentham matter in his life. There was no way he was putting his music in Wrentham's hands no matter how much he was willing to pay, and it was pretty clear already that that figure was nothing. Standing here, he was just wasting time.

"I'll pass, thanks." And for just a flash of an instant Zach got Wrentham's eyes to open up and actually see him. All it had taken was making it clear that the A and R man wasn't important to him. And finally Zach understood.

He'd missed the signs. Playing was supposed to be about the music. If it wasn't about the music, what was the point? He remembered the band in Santa Barbara. The guitarist managed a music store. The drummer laid tile. The bass player worked at the university. They played for kicks, for bragging rights, for the few extra bucks it brought them. It wasn't their life, it was their hobby.

He didn't see how he could do it.

And yet...

And yet he was chasing a phantom, he thought as he put away the Les Paul and rolled up his amp cord. The reality was, it wasn't going to happen for him, not now and probably not ever. Maybe what he'd had was all there was going to be—the odd festival appearance, a profile in a national music magazine, the well-received albums.

And playing in clubs where nobody there gave a damn, not even the A and R man.

He waited to see how it would feel, like touching a bruise to see how much it hurt. Curiously it didn't do more than ache. The reality was, he'd known it for some time. He just hadn't wanted to acknowledge it. Paige was what mattered. Paige was where he needed to go.

He picked up his guitar and his amp with a sigh. "Thanks, guys," he said to the session players. "Take care and good luck."

"HERE'S TO THE HAPPY couple!" The group crowded around the tables raised their glasses in a toast. Onstage, the guitarist broke into an impromptu version of Mendelssohn's wedding march.

Paige raised her champagne glass and clinked it against a dozen others.

They sat in McCall's for Kelly and Kev's Jack and Jill party. It had seemed like the perfect location back when she'd been involved in the planning. Although, she hadn't known then that she and Zach were going to be a thing of the past by the time the party happened. She hadn't anticipated the reminders everywhere she looked, hadn't realized she would ache so much even weeks later.

She'd heard that amputees sometimes had phantom pains in lost limbs for years.

Delaney leaned over to her. "Are you okay?"

She blinked a few times. "I'm fine. Just having a little allergy attack."

"What are you allergic to?"

Paige gave a smile that wobbled. "Electric guitars."

"Why didn't you stay home, honey?" Delaney asked gently. "All this is doing is reminding you of Zach."

"I wanted to be here for Kelly and Kev." She took another swallow of champagne.

"They're not going to care if you leave."

"I'll care," Paige said.

Delaney nodded. "Have you heard anything from him?"

"I don't know. I don't really check my messages much these days. I just don't want to deal with it."

"You're going to have to deal with it sooner or later."

"I'm dealing with it all the time," Paige said harshly. She looked down and rubbed a scuff on the wooden table. "I just don't want to let it take over. I mean, God, I knew him for a whopping four weeks. It was a fling, Delaney. In, out, done. Press Erase. Isn't that what you do?"

"Me, maybe. I don't know if you can."

"Maybe I'm different than I was."

"Maybe," Delaney agreed. "But not by that much."

"What do you want me to do about it?" Paige flared. "Sit around all weepy? Woe is me, I lost the guy who was the one? Because I—"

And the words locked up in her throat because Zach was standing there—in the doorway to the room. He wore jeans and a Red, Hot and Blue T-shirt and a motorcycle jacket. He looked unshaven and rough, as if he hadn't slept in a few days. He wasn't her type.

But he was breaking her heart.

Paige stared as he walked across the room to her. Her lips were numb, she realized, maybe even her entire body. Shock did that to a person, she dimly recalled. "What are you doing here?" she asked, voice barely audible.

"You're here."

"You're supposed to be in Nashville."

"Not anymore. Look, I'm sorry to interrupt, but I've tried your house a couple of times and this was the one place I remembered you'd be. I need to talk with you."

Onstage, the guitar wailed, giving voice to the emotions whirling through her. Out of the corner of her eye Paige could see everyone trying not to watch. She shoved her chair back and rose. "We are not going to do this here."

"What?"

"Whatever you've got in mind." She grabbed her jacket.

"This is a party. You want to talk, we take it outside." And without waiting for him, she walked out.

Fury buzzed through her. He had no right. He had no right to just show up like this. He had no right to put her through what he had and then try to get her to hope again.

She marched out to the street and whirled to face him. "What are you doing here, Zach?" she repeated. The wheels of passing cars hissed on the pavement

"I wanted to talk to you. To apologize."

"We've done this before," she said coolly. "I think last time it ended with you saying you wanted to be with me, which lasted just about, what, a week? Until you decided you didn't anymore."

Anger sparked in his eyes. "Don't put that on me. I never decided that. I told you from the beginning that I was coming back."

"As long as there wasn't anything more important going on." She balanced precariously on the line between anger and tears, struggling not to give in. Not in front of him. She stared hard at the streetlights instead.

"Look." Zach blew a breath out. "I screwed up. I blew it big time. I went hauling ass across the country for nothing when I should have stayed here with you. You're what I want. You're what matters to me. I came back here to tell you that."

She clapped her hands over her ears. "Cut the easy crap," she said to him, her voice high and thin. "You can't do this, you can't just come back here and do this. If you're going to be gone, stay gone."

"I can't do that. Look, I never meant to hurt you, Paige. I went back on the road because I had to. I had to give it one last try."

She hugged herself. "I know."

"Let me finish. It's always been home for me. But that was because I never had anyone who mattered before."

"You never let anyone matter."

"Maybe," he agreed. "But I let you. For the last two weeks I've sat out in a fleabag motel and missed you, just missed you and knocked my skull from a week till Sunday because I screwed this up. And I was an idiot to be three thousand miles away from you when all I wanted was to be right here. I don't want that life anymore, I want you."

"Until the next call from your manager, and then you'll go off again," she flung at him.

"No."

The quiet certainty in his voice stopped her. "Why?"

"Because I have something to stay home for. I'm coming back to L.A. I'm going to look for the session work, maybe even try producing."

And now that he wanted that, the room-and-board deal she'd offered was looking pretty good. "So is that an oblique way of asking if you can come move in? Pretend none of this ever happened?"

"No." He shook his head. "I don't want that. I want to be with you, Paige, but I want to do it the right way. And that means having my own place."

Bewildered, she looked at him. "I don't understand."

"I need to pull my own freight. If we're going to do this, I've got to move here, me, and I need to get a career going. And I want to see you while that's happening and, yeah, at some point I hope it works out that we do decide to get a place together. Our place, though. Not yours, not mine. Not me living off you. Does that make any kind of sense?"

"It costs a fortune to live here, Zach. What are you going to do, borrow money from Gloria?"

"Not really my style."

"Rob a bank?"

"No." He gave a try at a smile. "I sold the Les Paul, so the money from that will keep me for a couple of years, even out here."

It took a moment for the words to register. "The Les Paul? But…God, Zach, your guitar. Gloria gave that to you."

"She'll understand."

"She won't. It's irreplaceable."

"No." He stared at her. "Stuff can always be replaced. You can't."

"Zach, I—"

"I want to make this work, Paige," he said intensely. "That's what counts, not the damned guitar. Hell, it was part of the problem."

"This isn't about you giving up your music. It can't be. That's who you are."

"And I realized that the other night. I don't want to be out there pimping myself to get a contract. I want to be playing music, my music, and that means coming here and building a band. And if we only ever play family barbecues then that's what we do. Because I'll be sticking with what's real. And I'll be here with you. If you'll let me."

He broke off and reached out to touch her face. "I don't want anything from you except your time and a chance. I love you, Paige. I didn't know it until I was onstage looking at that idiot A and R guy and wondering what the hell I was doing in Nashville instead of with you." He swallowed. "You're what matters. Nothing else comes close. So come on, will you give it another go?"

She moistened her lips, afraid to hope. "Do you mean it?"

"Yeah, I mean it."

And she didn't remember moving after, but suddenly she was wrapped around him so tightly that she almost couldn't breathe, inhaling his scent, absorbing his feel, trying to understand that he was back, really back. "Zach, I love you. I figured it out the day you left, but I couldn't tell you."

"You could have told me," he murmured.

"Not then." She kissed him, hard. "I missed you so much."

"This road thing sucks," he said.

Paige leaned back and slanted a look at him. "Not entirely," she said. "Will you do something for me?"

He grinned. "Does it involve taking your clothes off?"

"Later," she said. "It involves going back inside."

"And what then?"

"Play me a song, Zach. I want you to play me a song."

He wrapped his arms around her and lifted her off her feet. "Wild Thing, I'll be your human jukebox for as long as you'll have me."

Laughing, she said, "Say it again, Zach, say it again."

* * * * *

Don't miss the next meeting of
SEX & THE SUPPER CLUB
Thea's story—Hot Moves
Coming in February 2007!

*Experience entertaining women's fiction for
every woman who has wondered
"what's next?" in their lives.
Turn the page for a sneak preview of
a new book from Harlequin NEXT,
WHY IS MURDER ON THE MENU, ANYWAY?
by Stevi Mittman*

On sale December 26, wherever books are sold.

Design Tip of the Day

Ambience is everything. Imagine eating a foie gras at a luncheonette counter or a side of coleslaw at Le Cirque. It's not a matter of food but one of atmosphere. Remember that when planning your dining room design.

—Tips from *Teddi.com*

"NOW THAT'S THE KIND of man you should be looking for," my mother, the self-appointed keeper of my shelf-life stamp, says. She points with her fork at a man in the corner of the Steak-Out Restaurant, a dive I've just been hired to redecorate. Making this restaurant look four-star will be hard, but not half as hard as getting through lunch without strangling the woman across the table from me. "*He* would make a good husband."

"Oh, you can tell that from across the room?" I ask, wondering how it is she can forget that when we had trouble getting rid of my last husband, she shot him. "Besides being ten minutes away from death if he actually eats all that steak, he's twenty years too old for me and— shallow woman that I am—twenty pounds too heavy. Besides, I am *so* not looking for another husband here. I'm looking to design a new image for this place, looking for some sense of ambience, some feeling, something I can build a proposal on for them."

My mother studies the man in the corner, tilting her head, the better to gauge his age, I suppose. I think she's grimacing, but with all the Botox and Restylane injected into that face, it's hard to tell. She takes another bite of her steak salad, chews slowly so that I don't miss the fact that the steak is a poor cut and tougher than it should be. "You're concentrating on the wrong kind of proposal," she says finally. "Just look at this place, Teddi. It's a dive. There are hardly any other diners. What does *that* tell you about the food?"

"That they cater to a dinner crowd and it's lunchtime," I tell her.

I don't know what I was thinking bringing her here with me. I suppose I thought it would be better than eating alone. There really are days when my common sense goes on vacation. Clearly, this is one of them. I mean, really, did I not resolve less than three weeks ago that I would not let my mother get to me anymore?

What good are New Year's resolutions, anyway?

Mario approaches the man's table and my mother studies him while they converse. Eventually Mario leaves the table with a huff, after which the diner glances up and meets my mother's gaze. I think she's smiling at him. That or she's got indigestion. They size each other up.

I concentrate on making sketches in my notebook and try to ignore the fact that my mother is flirting. At nearly seventy, she's developed an unhealthy interest in members of the opposite sex to whom she isn't married.

According to my father, who has broken the TMI rule and given me Too Much Information, she has no interest in sex with him. Better, I suppose, to be clued in on what they aren't doing in the bedroom than have to hear what they might be doing.

"He's not so old," my mother says, noticing that I have barely touched the Chinese chicken salad she warned me not to get. "He's got about as many years on you as you have on your little cop friend."

She does this to make me crazy. I know it, but it works all the same. "Drew Scoones is not my little 'friend.' He's a detective with whom I—"

"Screwed around," my mother says. I must look shocked, because my mother laughs at me and asks if I think she doesn't know the "lingo."

What I thought she didn't know was that Drew and I actually tangled in the sheets. And, since it's possible she's just fishing, I sidestep the issue and tell her that Drew is just a couple of years younger than me and that I don't need reminding. I dig into my salad with renewed vigor, determined to show my mother that Chinese chicken salad in a steak place was not the stupid choice it's proving to be.

After a few more minutes of my picking at the wilted leaves on my plate, the man my mother has me nearly engaged to pays his bill and heads past us toward the back of the restaurant. I watch my mother take in his shoes, his suit and the diamond pinkie ring that seems to be cutting off the circulation in his little finger.

"Such nice hands," she says after the man is out of sight. "Manicured." She and I both stare at my hands. I have two popped acrylics that are being held on at weird angles by bandages. My cuticles are ragged and there's marker decorating my right hand from measuring carelessly when I did a drawing for a customer.

Twenty minutes later she's disappointed that he

managed to leave the restaurant without our noticing. He will join the list of the ones I let get away. I will hear about him twenty years from now when—according to my mother—my children will be grown and I will still be single, living pathetically alone with several dogs and cats.

After my ex, that sounds good to me.

The waitress tells us that our meal has been taken care of by the management and, after thanking Mario, the owner, complimenting him on the wonderful meal and assuring him that once I have redecorated his place people will be flocking here in droves (I actually use those words and ignore my mother when she rolls her eyes), my mother and I head for the restroom.

My father—unfortunately not with us today—has the patience of a saint. He got it over the years of living with my mother. She, perhaps as a result, figures he has the patience for both of them, and feels justified having none. For her, no rules apply, and a little thing like a picture of a man on the door to a public restroom is certainly no barrier to using the john. In all fairness, it does seem silly to stand and wait for the ladies' room if no one is using the men's room.

Still, it's the idea that rules don't apply to her, signs don't apply to her, conventions don't apply to her. She knocks on the door to the men's room. When no one answers she gestures to me to go in ahead. I tell her that I can certainly wait for the ladies' room to be free and she shrugs and goes in herself.

Not a minute later there is a bloodcurdling scream from behind the men's room door.

"Mom!" I yell. "Are you all right?"

Mario comes running over, the waitress on his heels. Two customers head our way while my mother continues to scream.

I try the door, but it is locked. I yell for her to open it and she fumbles with the knob. When she finally manages to unlock and open it, she is white behind her two streaks of blush, but she is on her feet and appears shaken but not stirred.

"What happened?" I ask her. So do Mario and the waitress and the few customers who have migrated to the back of the place.

She points toward the bathroom and I go in, thinking it serves her right for using the men's room. But I see nothing amiss.

She gestures toward the stall, and, like any self-respecting and suspicious woman, I poke the door open with one finger, expecting the worst.

What I find is worse than the worst.

The husband my mother picked out for me is sitting on the toilet. His pants are puddled down around his ankles, his hands are hanging at his sides. Pinned to his chest is some sort of Health Department certificate.

Oh, and there is a large, round, bloodless bullet hole between his eyes.

FOUR NASSAU COUNTY police officers are securing the area, waiting for the detectives and crime scene personnel to show up. They are trying, though not very hard, to comfort my mother, who in another era would be considered to be suffering from the vapors. Less tactful in the twenty-first century, I'd say she was losing it. That is, if I didn't know her better, know she was milking it for everything it was worth.

My mother loves attention. As it begins to flag, she swoons and claims to feel faint. Despite four No Smoking signs, my mother insists it's all right for her to light up because, after all, she's in shock. Not to mention that signs, as we know, don't apply to her.

When asked not to smoke, she collapses mournfully in a chair and lets her head loll to the side, all without mussing her hair.

Eventually, the detectives show up to find the four patrolmen all circled around her, debating whether to administer CPR, smelling salts or simply call the paramedics. I, however, know just what will snap her to attention.

"Detective Scoones," I say loudly. My mother parts the sea of cops.

"We have to stop meeting like this," he says lightly to me, but I can feel him checking me over with his eyes, making sure I'm all right while pretending not to care.

"What have you got in those pants?" my mother asks him, coming to her feet and staring at his crotch accusingly. "*Baydar?* Everywhere we Bayers are, you turn up. You don't expect me to buy that this is a coincidence, I hope."

Drew tells my mother that it's nice to see her, too, and asks if it's his fault that her daughter seems to attract disasters.

Charming to be made to feel like the bearer of a plague.

He asks how I am.

"Just peachy," I tell him. "I seem to be making a habit of finding dead bodies, my mother is driving me crazy and the catering hall I booked two freakin' years ago for Dana's bat mitzvah has just been shut down by the Board of Health!"

"Glad to see your luck's finally changing," he says, giving me a quick squeeze around the shoulders before turning his attention to the patrolmen, asking what they've got, whether they've taken any statements, moved anything, all the sort of stuff you see on TV, without any of the drama. That is, if you don't count my mother's threats to faint every few minutes when she senses no one's paying attention to her.

Mario tells his waitstaff to bring everyone espresso,

which I decline because I'm wired enough. Drew pulls him aside and a minute later I'm handed a cup of coffee that smells divinely of Kahlúa.

The man knows me well. Too well.

His partner, whom I've met once or twice, says he'll interview the kitchen staff. Drew asks Mario if he minds if he takes statements from the patrons first and gets to him and the waitstaff afterward.

"No, no," Mario tells him. "Do the patrons first." Drew raises his eyebrow at me like he wants to know if I get the double entendre. I try to look bored.

"What is it with you and murder victims?" he asks me when we sit down at a table in the corner.

I search them out so that I can see you again, I almost say, but I'm afraid it will sound desperate instead of sarcastic.

My mother, lighting up and daring him with a look to tell her not to, reminds him that *she* was the one to find the body.

Drew asks what happened *this time*. My mother tells him how the man in the john was "taken" with me, couldn't take his eyes off me and blatantly flirted with both of us. To his credit, Drew doesn't laugh, but his smirk is undeniable to the trained eye. And I've had my eye trained on him for nearly a year now.

"While he was noticing you," he asks me, "did *you* notice anything about him? Was he waiting for anyone? Watching for anything?"

I tell him that he didn't appear to be waiting or watching. That he made no phone calls, was fairly intent on eating and did, indeed, flirt with my mother. This last bit Drew takes with a grain of salt, which was the way it was intended.

"And he had a short conversation with Mario," I tell him.

"I think he might have been unhappy with the food, though he didn't send it back."

Drew asks what makes me think he was dissatisfied, and I tell him that the discussion seemed acrimonious and that Mario looked distressed when he left the table. Drew makes a note and says he'll look into it and asks about anyone else in the restaurant. Did I see anyone who didn't seem to belong, anyone who was watching the victim, anyone looking suspicious?

"Besides my mother?" I ask him, and Mom huffs and blows her cigarette smoke in my direction.

I tell him that there were several deliveries, the kitchen staff going in and out the back door to grab a smoke. He stops me and asks what I was doing checking out the back door of the restaurant.

Proudly—because, while he was off forgetting me, dropping by only once in a while to say hi to Jesse, my son, or drop something by for one of my daughters that he thought they might like, I was getting on with my life—I tell him that I'm decorating the place.

He looks genuinely impressed. "Commercial customers? That's great," he says. Okay, that's what he *ought* to say. What he actually says is "Whatever pays the bills."

"Howard Rosen, the famous restaurant critic, got her the job," my mother says. "You met him—the good-looking, distinguished gentleman with the *real* job, something to be proud of. I guess you've never read his reviews in *Newsday*."

Drew, without missing a beat, tells her that Howard's reviews are on the top of his list, as soon as he learns how to read.

"I only meant—" my mother starts, but both of us assure her that we know just what she meant.

"So," Drew says. "Deliveries?"

I tell him that Mario would know better than I, but that I saw vegetables come in, maybe fish and linens.

"This is the second restaurant job Howard's got her," my mother tells Drew.

"At least she's getting *something* out of the relationship," he says.

"If he were here," my mother says, ignoring the insinuation, "he'd be comforting her instead of interrogating her. He'd be making sure we're both all right after such an ordeal."

"I'm sure he would," Drew agrees, then looks me in the eyes as if he's measuring my tolerance for shock. Quietly he adds, "But then maybe he doesn't know just what strong stuff your daughter's made of."

It's the closest thing to a tender moment I can expect from Drew Scoones. My mother breaks the spell. "She gets that from me," she says.

Both Drew and I take a minute, probably to pray that's all I inherited from her.

"I'm just trying to save you some time and effort," my mother tells him. "My money's on Howard."

Drew withers her with a look and mutters something that sounds suspiciously like "fool's gold." Then he excuses himself to go back to work.

I catch his sleeve and ask if it's all right for us to leave. He says sure, he knows where we live. I say goodbye to Mario. I assure him that I will have some sketches for him in a few days, all the while hoping that this murder doesn't cancel his redecorating plans. I need the money desperately, the alternative being borrowing from my parents and being strangled by the strings.

My mother is strangely quiet all the way to her house. She doesn't tell me what a loser Drew Scoones is—despite his good looks—and how I was obviously drooling over him. She doesn't ask me where Howard is taking me tonight or warn me not to tell my father about what happened because he will worry about us both and no doubt insist we see our respective psychiatrists.

She fidgets nervously, opening and closing her purse over and over again.

"You okay?" I ask her. After all, she's just found a dead man on the toilet and tough as she is that's got to be upsetting.

When she doesn't answer me I pull over to the side of the road.

"Mom?" She refuses to meet my eyes. "You want me to take you to see Dr. Cohen?"

She looks out the window as if she's just realized we're on Broadway in Woodmere. "Aren't we near Marvin's Jewelers?" she asks, pulling something out of her purse.

"What have you got, Mother?" I ask, prying open her fingers to find the murdered man's ring.

"It was on the sink," she says in answer to my dropped jaw. "I was going to get his name and address and have you return it to him so that he could ask you out. I thought it was a sign that the two of you were meant to be together."

"He's dead, Mom. You understand that, right?" I ask. You never can tell when my mother is fine and when she's in la-la land.

"Well, I didn't know that," she shouts at me. "Not at the time."

I ask why she didn't give it to Drew, realize that she wouldn't give Drew the time in a clock shop and add, "…or one of the other policemen?"

"For heaven's sake," she tells me. "The man is dead, Teddi, and I took his ring. How would that look?"

Before I can tell her it looks just the way it is, she pulls out a cigarette and threatens to light it.

"I mean, really," she says, shaking her head like it's my brains that are loose. "What does he need with it now?"

nocturne™

**WAS HE HER SAVIOR
OR HER NIGHTMARE?**

HAUNTED
LISA CHILDS

Years ago, Ariel and her sisters were separated for
their own protection. Now the man who vowed
revenge on her family has resumed the hunt, and
Ariel must warn her sisters before it's too late.
The closer she comes to finding them, the more
secretive her fiancé becomes. Can she trust the man
she plans to spend eternity with? Or has he been
waiting for the perfect moment to destroy her?

On sale December 2006.

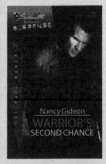

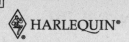

In February, expect **MORE**
from

HARLEQUIN® *Romance*®

as it increases to six titles per month.

What's to come...

Rancher and Protector

Part of the

Western Weddings

miniseries

BY JUDY CHRISTENBERRY

The Boss's
Pregnancy Proposal

BY RAYE MORGAN

REQUEST YOUR FREE BOOKS!

2 FREE NOVELS PLUS 2 FREE GIFTS!

HARLEQUIN®

Blaze®

Red-hot reads!

YES! Please send me 2 FREE Harlequin® Blaze® novels and my 2 FREE gifts. After receiving them, if I don't wish to receive any more books, I can return the shipping statement marked "cancel." If I don't cancel, I will receive 6 brand-new novels every month and be billed just $3.99 per book in the U.S., or $4.47 per book in Canada, plus 25¢ shipping and handling per book and applicable taxes, if any*. That's a savings of at least 15% off the cover price! I understand that accepting the 2 free books and gifts places me under no obligation to buy anything. I can always return a shipment and cancel at any time. Even if I never buy another book from Harlequin, the two free books and gifts are mine to keep forever.

151 HDN EF3W   351 HDN EF3X

Name _____ (PLEASE PRINT)

Address _____ Apt. _____

City _____ State/Prov. _____ Zip/Postal Code _____

Signature (if under 18, a parent or guardian must sign)

Mail to Harlequin Reader Service®:

IN U.S.A.	**IN CANADA**
P.O. Box 1867	P.O. Box 609
Buffalo, NY	Fort Erie, Ontario
14240-1867	L2A 5X3

Not valid to current Harlequin Blaze subscribers.

Want to try two free books from another line?
Call 1-800-873-8635 or visit www.morefreebooks.com.

---

* Terms and prices subject to change without notice. NY residents add applicable sales tax. Canadian residents will be charged applicable provincial taxes and GST. This offer is limited to one order per household. All orders subject to approval. Credit or debit balances in a customer's account(s) may be offset by any other outstanding balance owed by or to the customer. Please allow 4 to 6 weeks for delivery.

HB06

COMING NEXT MONTH

#297 BEYOND BREATHLESS Kathleen O'Reilly
The Red Choo Diaries, Bk. 1
When Manhattan trains quit and a sexy stranger offers to split the cost of a car, Jamie McNamara takes the deal. Now stuck in gridlock in a Hummer limo, she has hot-looking, hard-bodied Andrew Brooks across from her and nothing but time on her hands....

#298 LETTING LOOSE! Mara Fox
The Wrong Bed
He's buff. He's beautiful. He's taking off his clothes. And he's exactly what lawyer Tina Henderson needs. She's sure a wild night with a stripper will make her forget all about smooth attorney Tyler Walden. Only, there's more to "The Bandit" than meets the eye....

#299 UNTOUCHED Samantha Hunter
Extreme Blaze
Once Risa Remington had the uncanny ability to read minds, and a lot more.... Now she's lost her superpowers and the CIA's trust. The one thing she craves is human sexual contact. But is maverick agent Daniel MacAlister the right one to take her to bed?

#300 JACK & JILTED Cathy Yardley
Chloe Winton is one unmarried bride. Still, she asks, "Why let a perfectly good honeymoon go to waste?" So she doesn't. The private yacht that her former fiancé booked is ready and waiting. And so is its heart-stopping captain, Jack McCullough. Starry moonlit nights on the ocean make for quick bedfellows and he and Chloe are no exception, even with rocky waters ahead!

#301 RELEASE Jo Leigh
In Too Deep...
Seth Turner is a soldier without a battle. He's secreted in a safe house with gorgeous Dr. Harper Douglas, who's helping to heal his body. Talk about bedside manners... But can he fight the heated sexual attraction escalating between them?

#302 HER BOOK OF PLEASURE Marie Donovan
Rick Sokol discovers a pillow book of ancient erotic art, leading him to appraiser Megan O'Malley. The illustrated pages aren't the only thing Megan checks out, and soon she and Rick are creating a number of new positions of their own. But will their newfound intimacy survive when danger intrudes?

www.eHarlequin.com

HBCNM1206

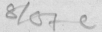